SLEIG ... H IT

A BILLIONAIRE

Bad Boys

HOLIDAY NOVELLA

max monroe

Sleighed It
A Bad Boy Billionaires Bonus Novella
Published by Max Monroe LLC © 2017, Max Monroe

ISBN-13: 978-1981496921
ISBN-10: 1981496920

Editing by Lisa Hollett, Silently Correcting Your Grammar (who adores us so. <3)
Formatting by Champagne Book Design
Cover Design by Perfect Pear Creative

DEDICATION

To our readers, this holiday season, we're thankful for a lot of things, but you are at the top of our list. Okay, you're second. But you're right below Oreos, so don't take it too personally.

We hope you get everything on your Christmas list this year—though, if it's something from us, you should probably plan on getting it in July. HAHA! Sorry.

To online shopping and Amazon Prime, thank you for catering to our laziness and never requiring us to wear bras or put on pants while doing our Christmas shopping this year. That's what *we* call a perfect holiday.

FOREWORD

By Kline Brooks

About a week ago, I received a package in the mail from Max and Monroe.

The wrapping was sloppy at best and torn at the edges—no doubt a rush job by one member of the lovable duo while they steered with their knee and pulled their coat tighter to hide the fact that they'd forgotten a bra while cruising down the highway. But inside—an area they'd obviously crafted with more care—lay a manuscript for a novella entitled *Sleighed It,* an oversized pink Post-it note stuck haphazardly to the top. A bad feeling washed over me instantly.

Kline,
We know you said you preferred to stay out of the limelight, and that you told us all about your most recent holiday adventures in confidence, but we couldn't help ourselves.
This one was too good not to share with our readers.
And since you are our swooniest male lead and a reader favorite, will you pretty please write the Foreword?

Just think about it, okay? No pressure.
Well, some pressure. Because we know our readers would love-love-love to hear from you.
Did we mention you're our favorite?
So, just read it, and then get the foreword to us by the end of this week. We've got a tight publishing schedule with this one, and our editor needs it soon. Oh, and promo started today.
But very little pressure.
Lots of love,
Max & Monroe

P.S. We went ahead and scheduled a photo shoot for you for the cover. We'll email you the details, but you should know we already paid the deposit, and some of us aren't billionaires.
P.P.S. Your masseuse told us you like light pressure, so really, you should thank us. It's like we're massaging you.

Needless to say, I wasn't left with a lot of options. When Max and Monroe want something, they're pretty demanding. It's like a prison camp filled with comedians, and the jokes keep coming until you come to heel or die. The fact that I just got back to the office from that fucking photo shoot is proof of that.

Fucking hell, Thatch is going to have a field day with this cover once it's released.

So now, here I sit, trying to figure out what in the hell to write for a Foreword.

I've read *Sleighed It*, in an effort to stir some sort of flow into my creative fountain for this thing, and despite the fact that I'll be on this cover strung up in Christmas lights and red velvet boxers, I enjoyed every second of it—maybe even more than when I was living it.

Probably because reading about it makes it easier to pretend it isn't me.

Max and Monroe spared no detail and provided no complimentary rose-colored glasses in their portrayal of me, my family, and my friends, but I assure you, after I read this novella, when my sheer disbelief and the PTSD from this year's holiday adventures dissipated, there was nothing left but a whole lot of love.

Life is a roller-coaster ride, but when you find that one person—or in my case, a whole group of batshit crazy people—to spend your days and nights with, the bumps and curves only provide you with more appreciation and thankfulness for the ride itself.

My wife, especially, is my world. Every day, I strive to be good enough for her, to be the man she deserves. Believe me, Georgia Brooks deserves a man who epitomizes good and honest and noble and kind.

I don't know that I'm all those things naturally, but she sure makes me try to be them for her.

My adorably awkward funny girl. The most loving, caring, and awe-inspiring mother to my two girls. A strong, ambitious, career-driven woman who can and will accomplish anything she sets her mind to.

And most importantly, my soul mate, *my person.*

Is it obvious I love her?

I sure fucking hope so. Because now that I'm done listing all the qualities she'd love to hear me list, I'm going to get real.

She is a fucking lunatic.

One with the sexiest ass and most show-stopping smile I've ever seen, but a lunatic all the same. Manically organized and anally hyper, she's an apple from her family's tree whether she likes to admit it or not.

And between keeping up with my wife's whims, running

Brooks Media, raising two spunky and precious girls, and Max Monroe writing the stories of our lives into their books, life has been crazy these past few years. Not to mention, Georgia's family splashed into the media after her brother Will starred in the popular reality docuseries *The Doctor Is In* and was dubbed Dr. *Obscene* to millions of viewers and never fully climbed back out.

It has been an absolute whirlwind, and recently, during this holiday season, my adorably zany wife craved peace and quiet and to spend a perfect Christmas without the added shenanigans of her family.

But what is a perfect Christmas?

Is it Georgia's meticulously planned-out dinner with flawlessly wrapped presents and the ambiance of a fire and softly playing holiday music?

Or is it merely spending the holiday season with the ones you love most?

I'd go to the ends of the earth to ensure my wife's happiness— insane, minutia-driven schedule or not. But for those who aren't so devotedly betrothed, the feeling might not be mutual.

My dear, beautiful, amazing readers, I invite you to turn the page and dive into another story of our lives. One that will no doubt bring you laughter and leave you with that deliriously happy and full-heart feeling Max Monroe is so good at giving.

The people you'll read about aren't perfect—but they're mine.

Happy Holidays, everyone.

All my love,

Kline Brooks

CHAPTER 1

It's the ~~Most Wonderful~~ Craziest Time of the Year

Georgia

Thanksgiving

"**S**hould I expect the usual suspects at dinner tonight?" Kline questioned from the driver's seat with a smirk, and immediately, I sighed.

Thick and dry, it was weightier than my normal sighs by about 2,500 pounds—roughly the cumulative mass of the band of relatives I was expecting to encounter imminently.

After spending the early afternoon eating a Thanksgiving lunch with Kline's parents, my day already felt twenty-six hours long, and, unfortunately for me, it was only five o'clock. *T-minus seven hours to go.*

"Considering it's Thanksgiving with my crazy a-s-s family, I imagine the whole gang will be there." Bad words had to be spelled out when your back seat had a curious five-year-old and an impressionable one-and-a-half-year-old ready to repeat anything that filled their little ears. Our friends Thatch and Cassie Kelly had already expanded my children's vocabulary enough for a lifetime.

My husband chuckled softly beside me, and I briefly considered taking my cuticle scissors out of my purse and stabbing his bubble of good humor repeatedly.

Don't get me wrong, I loved my family, but generally speaking, the holidays—any holiday—and my family didn't have a good track record. It was challenging enough getting through our monthly family dinners with my parents, but when extended relatives were involved, shit never failed to hit the proverbial fan. Bloody carnage where a finger used to be, septic backups, drunken Christmas tree tipping, and a near house fire thanks to a turkey in the deep fryer—you name it, we'd had it.

"Mommy! Mommy!" Julia called from the back seat. "Has it been ten minutes yet? Are we at Mimi and Papa's yet?"

Mimi and Papa, otherwise known as my mother and father, or Dick and Savannah Cummings, were two of my first-born daughter's favorite people on the planet. So much so that I often noticed her mimicking their behavior.

The first time I'd picked up on it, I'd nearly dropped dead in terror.

"Almost, sweetheart," I said evenly—even though I'd answered the same question fifteen times already. My calm exterior was a maternal façade. On the inside, I was slowly unraveling. A mother could only answer the same question so many times before she started to break. When the masking tape of propriety and lies holding me together gave way, everyone near me had better look out.

"Ugh! I'm tired of being in the car!" Julia whined again, and I shot venomous eyes at Kline.

You did this to me, they yelled. He smiled. *Bastard.*

What was it with children and car rides?

Or more than that, why did their sense of time always seem to move at warp speed?

Ten minutes equated to thirty seconds in their little minds.

Of course, Julia, my precocious and adorable five-year-old, was going through a bit of a stubborn phase that made all time seem painfully twisted, regardless of whether we were in the car or not. For the past six months or so, she couldn't let a moment pass without loudly voicing her disapproval when she did not like something—and she apparently didn't like much of anything anymore.

Seriously, guys, this little phase is driving me up the wall.
It's really bad *with a capital B and the word f-u-c-k-i-n-g in the front.*
Taking Julia on a trip to the grocery store? Forget about it. I might as well attempt to push a feral cat around in a cart filled with milk and tuna. And don't even get me started on what happens on the days she doesn't feel like going to school. Have you ever thought about what it would be like to get the little girl from The Exorcist *bathed, dressed, and ready to head out the door? Sounds pretty terrible, huh?*
My fellow moms, please pray for me. Lord knows I can't handle another thirteen years of little Miss Diva's attitude.

"Momma," Evie calmly announced from her rear-facing car seat sitting beside her sister.

"Yeah, baby?"

"Hi!" she exclaimed simply, snorting several giggles immediately after.

"Hi, Evie," I responded and silently thanked the heavens above that my littlest child was content being a calm and happy little lady—so far.

"Daddy!"

"Hi, Evie," Kline answered immediately, his blue eyes glimmering with love as he glanced in the rearview mirror at his two girls.

Our eighteen-month-old giggled in response and then exclaimed, "Lia! Lia! Lia! Lo youuuuuu, Lia!"

"Love you, Evie," Julia answered sweetly.

I guessed even little Miss Diva couldn't be annoyed by her baby sister's love.

I glanced behind me to find the girls holding hands, and my heart stretched tight with love. It was moments like these that reminded you why you wanted to be a parent in the first place. Between the chaos and stubborn phases and the sleepless nights, you could always count on those little, precious slivers of time where unconditional love for your children consumed you.

After all, God had to have something in place to prevent mother-on-child homicide and facilitate the survival of the human race.

The familiar tree-lined circular driveway and white brick of my parents' home came into view, and the sweet reminiscence of childhood memories and the stomach-clenching anxiety that always seemed to occur during the holidays hit me all at once. It was like whispering "home sweet home" and grabbing the "oh shit" handle at the same time.

"All right," Kline announced as he switched off the ignition. "We're here."

"Yay!" Julia shouted and immediately started unbuckling her own seat belt. "Mimi and Papa's!"

Kline turned toward me and placed his hand tenderly on my shoulder. "Ready?"

I shook my head, and he grinned.

"It'll be fine, Georgie," he reassured, but I called bullshit with a raise of my eyebrow.

"You and I both know holidays with my family never end fine."

Take last Christmas, for example. After we'd eaten turkey fried in beer—only my father, Dick Cummings, would be crazy enough to make another attempt at this after the fire of 2007—my entire family had proceeded to get into a screaming match about the inner workings of the *Twilight* series. Team Edward or Team Jacob might seem innocent enough, but what should have been a simple debate merely provided a domino effect into every issue we had ever had with one another. How a fictitious vampire love story served as a catalyst for an all-out family brawl was beyond me, but the night had ended with half of my family storming out before the presents were even opened and Julia crying the whole way home.

Disaster, I tell you. It was always a fucking disaster.

"If anyone brings up *Twilight* or your uncle Donnie tries to discuss politics or, God forbid, your aunt Rhonda tries to sell us items from her most recent pyramid scheme, I'll be the first to get the girls packed up, and we'll blow this popsicle stand."

See? Even my husband doesn't want to relive the Twilight *fiasco of last year.*

"Promise?"

Kline slid a loose lock of hair behind my ear and kissed my cheek. "Promise, baby."

"Let's go! Let's go! Get me outta here!" Julia screeched as her little hands went apeshit on the child-locked back door.

"Love you," my husband whispered through the pounding beat of my rapidly escalating blood pressure. He pressed a quick peck to my lips before hopping out of the driver's seat and unleashing the caged animal—aka our five-year-old—from the back seat.

Quick as a whip, Julia sprinted across the driveway until she reached the stoop of my parents' front door and started a secondary assault on its—thankfully—solid wood.

At a much more normal pace, I slid out of the passenger seat and unbuckled Evie from her car seat. She smiled a full-toothed grin and wrapped her little hands around my neck as I lifted her out of the car.

Two seconds later, her little hands reached out for her father, and he happily pulled her into his arms. Evie was a total daddy's girl. I couldn't blame her, though; I loved my husband something fierce too. Always doting, always tender, and never failing to show his love, Kline Brooks was the best father and husband a woman could ask for. If anyone was lucky in our relationship, it was for sure me.

By the time we reached the door, my dad already had Julia on his hip and a big grin slung across his face. "Savannah! The Brookses are here!" he called behind him, and my mother's face appeared over his shoulder mere seconds later.

"Happy Thanksgiving!"

"Mimi!" Julia squealed and hopped into her grandmother's arms.

"Oh my goodness, I swear you've grown two inches and gotten even prettier since the last time I saw you!"

Julia giggled. "You sos silly, Mimi! You just saws me yesterdays!"

Don't ask me why, but my five-year-old had a thing for adding the letter S to the majority of her words, even the non-plural ones. And no, it wasn't the product of a lisp. These S's were completely voluntary and random in their timing—at least, I hadn't been able to discern a pattern.

My mom smiled and kissed her oldest granddaughter on the

nose before setting her to her feet. With Evie now being carried by my dad, Julia ran into the foyer, and the rest of us followed behind.

I guess it's not off to too bad of a start...

Kline smiled down at me as he wrapped his arm around my shoulder and led us into the living room. The instant we stepped into the room, we were greeted with hellos and happy Thanksgiving wishes from everyone sitting around the fire and television that was currently blaring a football game.

I looked around the room and took stock. The usual suspects—as my husband so eloquently described them—were, in fact, *all here.*

Granny Cummings. Uncle Donnie, Aunt Rhonda, and their four sons—and my cousins—Randy, Ralphie, Ricky, and Raymond. Two of whom were married and had their spouses with them.

Is it obvious my aunt Rhonda really likes names that start with R?
And dick?
Four kids, guys.

Dick and Savannah's cozy living room was packed. I silently prayed everyone would be on their very best and disaster-free behavior.

"Where's Will and Melody and my favorite niece?" I asked once I realized my brother and his family were nowhere to be found. We needed them to stabilize the normalcy equilibrium!

"Dr. Obscene won't make it tonight," my father answered loudly as he cleared Randy and Ricky out of the way and plopped down onto the couch. The man had no filter, and ever since Will had starred in *The Doctor Is In*—a crazy-popular reality docuseries about his career as an obstetrician, good ol' Dick wouldn't let the outrageous nickname die.

"Will is on call tonight," my mom kindly added, "so they stopped by earlier for a light Thanksgiving lunch with your dad and me."

That bastard! He probably wasn't even on call. He just didn't want to deal with the insanity that followed our father's side of the family around like a fucking tail.

I pulled my cell phone out of my purse and sent my traitor brother a quick text.

Me: You dirty liar! You're not even on call, are you? You're just putting your sanity above mine like a narcissist.

Will: Reread that text and tell me who sounds like the real narcissist. Happy Thanksgiving, Georgie! Love you!

Me, self-centered? As if!

Me: Let me guess, you're on call for Christmas too...

Will: Well...

Me: I kind of hate you right now, William.

Will: Love you too, Gigi!

Me: Ugh. Give Mel and my favorite niece a kiss for me.

Will: No kiss for me?

Me: Shove off.

Will: Advice: Don't stay past dessert. Uncle Donnie started

drinking as soon as he got there—right as we were leaving—four hours ago. We both know Uncle Donnie, and that much beer makes for a bad combination.

Me: If it were up to me, I wouldn't stay past appetizers.

Will: Hahahahahahaha

Me: Shut up, asshole.

My brother was always my buffer at these shindigs. If Granny started hounding me about something ridiculous, I'd just mention something awful Will had done. And when Uncle Donnie passed beer number ten, I'd throw Will into the pit of doom like a virgin sacrifice and run.

How in the hell was I going to survive without him?

We had been at my parents' for all of twenty minutes when the first flood of anxiety overflowed my veins, spilling out into my body and urging that claustrophobic, eye-twitchy sensation I'd come to associate with holidays and my family.

Uncle Donnie was currently motorboating Aunt Rhonda in the kitchen while Dick and Savannah looked on. They'd made a bet that the action didn't actually make the sound of a marine motor, and Uncle Donnie had set about proving them wrong. Raymond followed his wife past the doorway, currently blocking my view, thankfully, but then started humping the air behind her. Ricky and Ralphie snickered from their spot on the fireplace hearth.

"How much longer do we need to be here?" I whispered to my husband behind gritted teeth. He just grinned, wrapped his arm around my shoulders, and tucked me into his side.

"Baby, we haven't even eaten dinner yet."

"I know, but maybe we can make up an excuse to leave early," I whispered back. "Maybe I can convince Julia to act like she's sick so we all have to leave?"

Kline raised an amused brow.

"Fine," I sighed. "I won't bring our five-year-old into it. But I know I can definitely fake a stomach bug."

It was sad that on Thanksgiving, a day meant to remind us of all of our blessings and the wonderful things in our lives, I was silently wondering if there was some type of fake emergency I could come up with so that Kline, the girls, and I could escape without trauma but…did I mention my uncle's face was fully seated in my aunt's breasts?

"Georgia," Kline whispered in my ear, a little laugh roughening his mostly smooth voice, "I love you endlessly, and I can sense your desperation, but you and I both know you're a shit liar. We'd never make it out of here unquestioned."

I frowned dramatically.

"Not to mention, even though your family is batshit crazy, we shouldn't dip out on them in the middle of Thanksgiving."

Why did my husband have to be so fucking noble all the time?

Normally, it was one of my favorite qualities of his, but not today. Today, I needed him to be less magnanimous and more let's get the fuck out of here.

I groaned, and he only held me tighter, a small smirk kissing his lips.

While Julia and Evie appeared content with playing Barbies on the floor of the living room—mercifully oblivious to the orgy in the kitchen—I silently tried my damnedest to be thankful our girls weren't screaming and pulling each other's hair out and find my happy place.

Only growing up with a brother, I'd realized quickly with my two girls that sisters were an enigma—one minute fighting, and the next the best of friends. You never knew what you were going to get.

"Georgia, honey," my mother beckoned me from the kitchen. I turned slowly, peeking minutely out one eye to try to avoid further scarring myself for life. Luckily, the only pie in sight was pumpkin, and my mother was sliding it gracefully into the oven.

"Yes?"

"Mind pouring Granny another glass of wine?"

I glanced back to the recliner in the other corner of the living room to find my Granny guzzling the rest of the wine in her glass, her lips already stained a deep purple from who fucking knows how many glasses of Merlot she'd already consumed.

Her eyes met mine, and she raised her glass in the air. "Snap, snap, Georgie."

Hell's bells. Granny was drunk, and we hadn't even started dinner yet.

"Sure thing, Granny," I muttered and left Kline in the living room to walk into the kitchen and grab my father's eighty-eight-year-old mother more booze.

Upon arrival in the kitchen, I noticed something far scarier than my aunt and uncle's PDA—my mother's normal display of food was nonexistent. I glanced around the counters feverishly, but they were startlingly empty. No mashed potatoes or stuffing or turkey or any and all of the other delicious food staples that signified Thanksgiving dinner.

"Uh…do you need help with anything, Mom?" I asked, and she shook her head as she pulled the cork on a fresh bottle of Merlot.

Fuck, I hoped Granny hadn't already finished off bottle number one by herself. She was known for having a loose and inappropriate mouth once alcohol came into play, and my cousins would do nothing more than egg her on.

"Nope." She shook her head. "Granny insisted on handling Thanksgiving dinner this year."

I looked around the empty counters again, my skepticism growing. I didn't see any fucking food.

"Apparently," my mom went on, "she managed to get a very famous New York chef to make our dinner. Isn't that a wonderful treat this year?"

A renowned chef dropping everything to cook dinner for my family on Thanksgiving of all days? It all sounded pretty fucking sketchy if you asked me.

Growing agitated at the thought of no food to cut the effects of all the booze, I took a quick glance into the dining room, where only empty dishes, glasses, plates, and cutlery sat. "Uh…okay…but…where is the chef, and where the hell is the food?"

"Granny said the food will be delivered at six p.m. on the dot."

I squinted in confusion. "So…who exactly is this famous chef?"

My mother shrugged. "I'm not sure, but I thought it was really thoughtful of Granny to offer to handle the food this year. It's been nice not having to spend the whole day cooking. Your father has quite enjoyed it too," she added and waggled her eyebrows. "He definitely worked up an appetite for Thanksgiving this morning *and* this afternoon."

"Hell yes!" Uncle Donnie cheered, slapping my father with a resounding high five.

It was times like these that I wished I had one of those marm-y moms that were uptight and could barely spell the word sex, much less say anything about sex out loud. But that wasn't my reality. Savannah Cummings was a certified sex therapist and world-renowned over-sharer.

"Wow. Thanks, Mom. That's exactly what I wanted to be thinking about right before dinner."

She waved me off with a grin. "Sex and intimacy are good for the soul and your marriage, honey. Speaking of which, how are things between you and Kline? Is the sex still—"

"Everything's good, Mom." I cut her off and held up Granny's newly filled glass of wine. "I better get this glass of Merlot to Granny before she starts yelling at my kids about empty glasses being for pansy-asses."

Honestly, I didn't know which was worse: feeding Granny more booze, or talking about new-age sex positions with my mother. It seemed like a lose-lose situation to me, and the only obvious option was self-preservation. Granny was a grown-ass woman, and if she wanted to get all boozed up and spout nonsense during dinner, that was her business. I'd just have to pray no one else's "nonsense," as she put it, pushed her out of control.

"Here, Gran," I said and carefully handed her the glass.

"Geez, it took you long enough," she muttered. "I thought I might die of old age before you made it in here."

Boy, my granny is only getting sweeter with each passing year.

I forced a smile to my lips and moved to the opposite side of the room, far away from the crotchety old lady guzzling wine. Finding a spot between Kline and my father, I attempted to enjoy the football game, and from the looks of it, Seattle was kicking Minnesota's ass.

I'd never been a huge fan of professional football, but ever since I'd started working as the Mavericks' Director of Marketing, I'd grown to enjoy it. Well, at least more than I used to. To be honest, I still didn't really understand the game, but I sure as shit knew how to market the team. When it came to filling the stadium with fans and gaining new endorsements for my players, I'd become a goddamn professional.

But understanding the game itself was more of a work in progress—one that might take eternity to complete.

Sure seems like I need some Team Edward now.

"You idiots! What are you doing!" my uncle Donnie shouted toward the television while my dad cheered. "Yes! That's it!"

As a result, venomous looks were exchanged.

Dick and Donnie were diehard fans for whatever team the other hated. It didn't matter who was playing or that nothing of actual substance was at stake, my dad and his brother cheered for their chosen team like they'd been fans their entire lives.

"Man, it's not looking good for your boys, Don. Your quarterback might as well be standing around with his dick in his hands."

"Shut up, Dick!"

My dad just grinned, loving every damn minute of his brother's misery. It was a lifelong urge for brotherly competition that wouldn't die until they did. Unfortunately for everyone else in the house, it oftentimes turned ugly.

Donnie jumped as his player went down, and I flinched unconsciously as visions of a sporting match of our own—though, less football and more blood sport—played out in my head.

For the love of God, Dad, stop taunting Uncle Donnie...he's got four giant sons as backup, and all you've got is me.

Just as a commercial break finally eased the tension in the room—as well as the knot in my chest—the doorbell rang.

Fluffing great. Who's this now?

Granny hooted, slamming the recliner down and startling my attention to her. A smile curved her lips as she glanced at her watch. "Six o'clock on the dot! Dinner is here!"

Curious, and still skeptical—read: terrified—about the dinner situation, I hopped out of my seat and headed into the entry with my grandmother not too far behind.

A young, twentysomething man stood on the front porch

with way too much innocence. He didn't look at all how I'd imagined a renowned chef in New York City did. He'd need twenty more layers of wrinkles and badassery. My brow pinched nervously. "Hello, my name is Michael, and I have a Meals on Wheels delivery for a—" he paused for a brief moment and glanced at his clipboard "—Sadie Cummings."

I'm sorry, had he just said Meals on Wheels? As in, the food delivery service for the elderly and disabled?

My gaze moved to his fleece jacket, the logo threaded carefully into the right side of his chest.

Ah, fucking hell.

My granny had just illegally utilized a humanitarian community resource for our Thanksgiving dinner.

Famous NYC chef my ass. I knew it didn't add up!

"That's me," Granny said proudly. "You are just on time!"

"Just sign here, ma'am." Michael held out his clipboard, and gladly, Granny signed on the dotted line. "If you give me a minute, I'll grab everything from the truck."

"Just carry it on in, Michael." Granny waved her hand generously toward the entryway. "We've got a hungry house waiting to dig in!"

Her voice held more affection for Michael than it had for me.

When he chuckled and jogged for his truck, I knew why. He humored her *and* moved at a brisk pace. Not to mention, he clearly wasn't bothered by the goddamn scheme my grandmother had running here.

At a complete loss for what to say, I followed Michael's lead down the hall and into the kitchen as he carried in the first box of food.

"Look, Mom," I announced, and sarcasm dripped from my voice like honey. "Granny ordered us Thanksgiving on Wheels."

Savannah's head came up slowly and then all at once as she

noticed the Meals on Wheels insignia on the box. "Oh my."

Yeah, *oh my* was right.

"Dinner is served, everyone!" Granny proudly announced to everyone in the living room as Michael finished filling the kitchen island with several more boxes and took his leave.

Lucky bastard.

"Actually," my mother chimed in as she opened up a box to find individual meal trays labeled with heating instructions, "it's not served…*yet.*"

"What's going on, Vanna?" Dick was happy to stay uninvolved until dinner got delayed. Now he had fucks, and he was ready to fucking give them.

"Well, *Dick…*" My mother's voice walked an impressive line between polite calm and *I'll fuck your shit up real good.* "Your mother generously ordered us Meals on Wheels for Thanksgiving. And it's going to take another—" she glanced down at one of the trays "—twenty minutes before dinner will be hot and ready."

"Oh!" Julia exclaimed excitedly once she plopped her little butt on a barstool and started browsing through our dinner trays. "I wants the ones with Jell-Os and chocolate puddings!"

Fucking hell. It was one of those "easy chew" trays!

"Me too," Randy offered, giving my five-year-old a steely, competitive brow. Out of the corner of my eye, I noticed Kline stepping a little closer, just in case he had to protect her.

Jesus Christmas.

My appetite was officially lost. The combination of guilt over eating something that should've been delivered to people who actually needed it and social anxiety at the hands of my family was a potent suppressant.

"Everyone go back into the living room, enjoy the rest of the game, and I'll get these meals heated up," my mother ordered with a wave of her hand.

"Already on it, Savannah!" Donnie chimed in as he stepped back inside the French doors that led to the back deck. "I went ahead and fired up the grill and put a few meals on the barbie!" he exclaimed and then proceeded to crack up at himself.

My mother's eyes darted to my father, who had already made himself comfortable on the couch again. "Dick, honey, did you happen to fix the gas on that grill?"

It took a whole two seconds before my dad shot out of his recliner and to his feet. But by the time he reached the deck doors, it was too late. Flames of gold and orange and red filled our normally wooded view from the window.

"Oh my God!" my mother and I shouted at the same time.

"Oh! Fireworks!" Julia cheered and started to hop off her barstool. "I wants to go outside and sees the fireworks!"

"No," Kline stated firmly, swooping our daughter off her feet and into his arms. "Those aren't fireworks, sweetie. Let's you, me, and Evie go play in the front yard."

He moved swiftly down the front hall, and I was thankful. The language was about to go foul in here, and I wasn't convinced some of it wouldn't be from my very own mouth.

My cousins and their wives looked on with smiles—the fucking lunatics. It was like they actually *liked* this shit.

"Goddammit, Donnie! The whole fucking deck is gonna go up in flames!" Dick shouted at his brother on the deck.

"Don't be so fucking dramatic, Dick! It's just a little fire!"

"A little fire, my ass! Vanna call 9-1-1!"

"Happy fucking Holidays," I muttered to myself, but Granny overheard and started into a rolling, choking chuckle.

Thanksgiving on Wheels and an actual explosion on the deck—it was definitely the holidays with my family.

Once the fire department had given my parents the all clear and assured them there was no damage to the house itself—thankfully, Dick had managed to break out the fire extinguisher and keep flames down to a dull roar—and that they didn't need to stay in a hotel for the evening, Kline and I packed up the girls and headed home.

During the drive, I couldn't stop myself from wondering what Christmas would be like.

My eyes stung as all different scenarios—all equally fucking awful—assaulted me.

God, I just wanted to enjoy a good Christmas this year. A perfect Christmas. A Hallmark card-worthy holiday with Kline and the girls.

Everyone smiling and the house decorated beautifully with a gorgeous display of food on the table. Perfectly wrapped presents underneath the tree, a fire burning brightly, and children excitedly opening gifts while the adults looked on with hot cocoa mugs and loving smiles.

That's what I wanted.

I didn't think it was too much to ask for.

Without second-guessing myself, I pulled my phone out of my purse and texted my two best friends.

Me: What do you guys think about sneaking away to our cabin in the Catskills for Christmas this year? Just the six of us and the kids.

About a year and a half ago, Kline and I had purchased this gorgeous cabin in the Catskills. We'd bought it shortly after Evie was born, with our little family of four in mind, and it'd quickly become our home away from home getaway.

It was nestled in the hills, and the views from the wraparound deck and porch were absolutely breathtaking. Especially during the winter months, when the sights and sounds of snow filled the air and surrounded the cabin. Not to mention, it wasn't short on bedrooms, bathrooms, or space. It could easily fit our closest friends and still have plenty of room.

But most importantly, it was a disaster-free zone.

Hence, the perfect place to spend Christmas.

Cassie: Let me guess. Thanksgiving with your family ended in its usual traumatic fashion.

Me: Granny ordered Meals on Wheels for our dinner, and Uncle Donnie set my parents' deck on fire.

Cassie: Fluffing hell, Granny Cummings cracks my ass up.

Winnie: Oh, shit. Is everyone okay?

Me: Yeah. Everyone is fine. Crazy. But fine.

Me: So, Christmas in the Catskills? Please say yes. Please say yes.

Cassie: I'm game.

Winnie: I'll have to work around the Mavericks game schedule, but I'm in too.

Me: YES! Come over to my house Saturday night for dinner, and we'll plan it all out?

Cassie: I'll be there.

Winnie: Me too.

Me: I LOVE YOU GUYS.

And that was that. This year, we'd spend Christmas with our closest friends.

No disasters. No fights. No fires. Just our friends, the gorgeous Catskills mountain views, and a nice little Christmas in our cabin.

It sounded like perfection to me.

And you can bet your sweet ass, I'd make goddamn sure everything ran smooth as silk.

CHAPTER 2

It's Beginning to Look a Lot Like ~~Christmas~~ Anxiety

Kline

December 18th Morning

I awoke with a start, and my eyes scanned the room, striving to grasp at familiarity and focus. The walls of our bedroom were already lit with the morning light of the sun.

Shit. The sun doesn't come up until fucking noon—only a slight exaggeration, by the way—this time of year. I almost didn't even want to know what time it was.

Still, I guessed I was part masochist because I rubbed at my eyes and glanced at the clock on the nightstand beside me anyway.

8:12 a.m. About two fucking *hours* later than I normally woke up on weekday mornings.

Georgia turned onto her side, her eyes still closed, but her hand already reaching out for me. Soft and warm, her fingers slid down my bare chest to my abdomen until they reached the skin just above the waistband of my briefs.

I stopped her movements before they made it to a place I wouldn't be able to resist.

"We don't have time, Benny. We gotta get moving. It's already past eight."

Completely ignoring my rebuttal, my wife giggled and stretched her leg over my waist until she was sitting up and straddling my hips. Before I found the willpower to stop her, her devious fingers moved my briefs out of the way, releasing my now hardened cock from its cotton restraint.

Surprisingly—and deliciously—bare underneath her night-shirt, she rubbed herself against me until I was sporting more than just morning wood.

Fuck me. Bare pussy. I groaned and pretended to pretend to think about resisting. I mean, I needed to be in the office.

With a slow and seductive roll of her hips, she slid my cock inside of her.

It was like she'd heard my silent prayer—the one where I spent the morning fucking my wife, not the one I was pretending to have about making it to work in a timely fashion.

"Georgia."

"*Kline*," she mocked me—fucking me at the same time. Maybe it made me twisted, but I had to admit I liked it.

"We're going to be late for work."

"I don't care." She smiled like the devil and moaned as her head fell back. The tips of her long, blond locks brushed across my thighs.

"My boss is a real prick."

She laughed at my obvious lie—being that the boss was me—and shook her head.

"I *have* heard that about him, but you'll just have to deal with his wrath."

"I really do have a meeting with that film production company this morning."

"Still don't care."

She rolled her hips, and my vision blurred. *Good God, I have never cared about work less in my life.*

"I'm pretty sure you also have a morning meeting…" I went on, content to play the game if it made her work harder to get my attention—attention that was *so* already gotten.

"I. Don't. Care." Up and down, she moved her hips, pleasuring herself on my cock. "I need this, Kline. Please," she begged. I almost broke character at the begging, and I wasn't the only one. My cock was about to go off-script and write his own ending if she didn't get herself off pretty quickly. I watched, entranced, as she pulled her nightshirt over her head and tossed it to the floor.

I had a feeling Georgia was using this good-morning sex as a way to alleviate anxiety. She'd been so focused on making sure our little family and friends had the best Christmas in the Catskills next week that I was starting to worry she would drive herself crazy.

I probably should've tried to get her to talk about it instead of giving in to the fucking, but the day I could resist my beautiful, sexy, fucking amazing wife, I'd be ten feet in the ground and without a pulse.

Maybe just talk after the sex.

Yeah. That was a good idea. I'd talk to her about it after the sex.

The delicious. Perfect. Mind-blowing sex with my wife…

I groaned, and I couldn't stop myself from arching my back and sliding deeper inside of her. Warm, soft, tight. Being inside of my wife was honestly heaven on earth.

Reaching out my hands, I gripped her waist and took the lead. Not too slow. Not too fast. But so wonderfully fucking deep. Good Lord, I loved being buried inside of her perfect cunt.

"Yes. Thank God," she moaned and braced herself with her hands on my chest. A slow and seductive smile curled her lips, and I couldn't take my eyes off of the goddess sitting above me.

I stared at her eyes. Blue. Heated.

I stared at her lips. Soft and parted and wet.

I stared at the lush curves of her perfect tits and tiny waist.

And when my gaze caught sight of the wedding band resting on her finger, a new pulse of pleasure ran through me. Mine. This gorgeous, sexy creature was all fucking mine.

I flipped her onto her back and pushed myself to the hilt.

Heaven. Fucking heaven.

Then I did it again.

And again.

And again.

Georgia's moans grew breathier, longer, and deeper until her tight cunt came all over my cock, her body arching inside my arms and her nails finding their way up my back and into my scalp.

She felt too good. Too warm. Too fucking perfect. And I'd been skirting the line of blowing my load since the moment she'd sunk down on me.

I was officially done.

I didn't last another minute and came deep inside my wife with a groan.

"Okay, so I just need the tents, chairs, lanterns, sparklers, and the ingredients for the cupcakes. I could swing by the sporting goods store right after work and then head to the grocery and the specialty bakery," my wife muttered to herself as she struck off item after item on her to-do list and added two more for every one she removed.

"Georgie, baby?" I called, my forehead wrinkled in confusion as my hands worked to finish knotting my tie.

"Yes?" she answered distractedly, still looking at her list.

"Am I missing something?"

"What do you mean?" I waited patiently for her eyes to leave the paper and meet my own, and eventually—about fifteen seconds later—she didn't disappoint.

"What do you mean, Kline?" she asked, sassy this time. She didn't like that I was wasting her time with things like eye contact.

"I mean…our cabin has furniture. Bedrooms. Electricity. Pretty sure you don't need to pack tents, chairs, and lanterns."

She rolled her eyes. Apparently, I was *so* not in the know. "They're not those kind of chairs, and the tents aren't to sleep in. They're for the Chinese lantern release I have planned one night."

"Chinese lantern release?" My eyebrows inched toward my hairline.

She sighed. "Just show up."

"Okay," I agreed, officially done asking questions. "Show up, I could. Show up, I would," I remarked in my best Yoda voice.

She cracked a little smile just as our oldest came skidding into the kitchen like she was at the end of a zip line.

"Mom! I'm hungrys! I want Eggos!"

Georgia looked harried immediately, so I stepped in. "I got this, Mom."

She turned grateful eyes on me immediately, but I was already en route to the freezer.

"Blueberry or plain?" I asked my angel, slathering my voice with disgust on the word plain.

She giggled and cheered, "Blueberrys!"

I grabbed the appropriate box out of the freezer and popped a couple of waffles in the toaster before walking over to Evie in the high chair and blowing a kiss at her. She giggled and tried to catch it. "And what about you, princess? What can I get you this morning?"

"She already ate," Georgia commented. I turned to look at her, but her face was still aimed directly at the list.

"Baby, why don't *you* eat breakfast? I'll fix you something."

She was shaking her head before I even finished speaking.

"Christmas is in a week, and we leave in four days. This stuff has to get done!"

"I know what else has to get done."

Her eyes turned venomous as they actually met mine. "Ugh. Don't remind me."

"Georgie—"

"I'm doing it today, okay? You can get off my back."

I laughed at her theatrics. I'd barely even mentioned the fact that she'd yet to tell her parents we wouldn't be spending Christmas with them. But I wanted to make sure she fit it on her list somewhere instead of standing them up. I'd broken the news to my parents fairly easily. Of course, they had a habit of spending this holiday in the Caribbean anyway. But still, she needed to do it.

"I was just reminding you."

"Well…thanks. I guess that's nice." The tone of her voice said she didn't think I was nice at all. I hid my smirk behind my mug of coffee. "Here," she said, grabbing a piece of paper from the bottom of her pile and shoving it to the side for me to read. "My email to Savannah. Give it a look, and let me know if you think I can send it as-is."

I plucked the paper from the surface of the counter and had almost started to read when she added, "Which I hope you do. I don't have time to draft another."

O-kay. *Note to self: Don't suggest any changes unless she refers to her mother as an overly sexualized Joseph Stalin or the like.*

Dearest Savannah and Dick,

I rolled my eyes, but I resisted the urge to comment and kept reading.

I regret to inform you that we'll be unable to attend family Christmas this year. As much as you know I enjoy blood sport, injuries, and easy-chew meals, I've decided to go a different direction this year. I'm not "on call" like Will, but we will be otherwise occupied. We wish you the happiest of holidays and will see you the week after to celebrate.
Thanks for your understanding,
Georgia Rose Brooks (and family)

Wow. Okay.

It was both honest and vague, and I couldn't quite put my finger on how to tell her she might want to take a second look.

"Georgie..." I muttered, and her head shot up, fire blazing in her eyes in direct challenge. Upon witnessing all that hostility, I treaded carefully.

"What?" she snapped when I took too long to form words.

"It's..."

"It's...what?"

"Maybe you should do a second draft—"

"It's my fifteenth."

Looking at my wife, seeing how desperately she wanted this Christmas to be different, I made a command decision to let it ride. Dick and Savannah were adults, and knowing them, they would probably get a kick out of all the things that might be perceived as insults by someone else.

"It's perfect. Send away."

"Thanks, Kline," she said, her body melting, her voice soft, her eyes loving.

I leaned forward and touched my lips to hers.

"You're welcome, love. Though, I wouldn't completely count out an easy-chew meal in your future." It took her a minute and a wink from me to get it.

"Oh, gross!" she yelled through a laugh. "Jesus, get out of here and go to work, would you?"

I smiled and slipped around her, dragging a hand across her hip before grabbing my keys off the counter, tossing them in the air, and catching them on the drop. "You know, I think I will go to work. At least Dean would appreciate the creativity in that statement," I teased.

"Goodbye!" she retorted with a finger wave.

I laughed all the way out of the house. But even more important, through listening carefully, I knew she kept giggling just as long.

I was almost into the city when my phone rang. I'd made a pledge not to look at my phone while driving—even to see who was on the caller ID—so I hit the button to answer and use hands-free on my steering wheel.

"Hello?"

"Well, goooood morning, Klinehole!" Thatch's voice boomed over the sound system of my car. I almost groaned.

"You sure sound chipper this morning," I remarked, forgoing a formal greeting since I knew my ridiculous friend didn't want one anyway. He wanted the attention to go to him as quickly as possible.

"Cassie gave me a morning blowie, and I swear my balls are still tingling."

"Jesus Christ, that's entirely too much information."

"Wow. Grumpy much? I think we can safely rule out your having gotten a morning blow—"

I rolled my eyes and cut in. "Thatch, the point of your call?"

"What? A friend can't just phone a friend in the morning? Are we so past traditional pleasantries that I have to have a reason for my call? By God, I'm insulted. We've been friends for nearly half a century, and my devotion is unquestionable. What makes you think—"

"Shut up!" I broke in. "Stop bullshitting me, and get to the point."

"You know, Kline," Thatch said with a chuckle over the speakers. "This is why I like you so much. You don't take bullshit, and you don't waste time. You get right to the heart of the matter and don't back down when the rest of us circle it. I—"

"I'm *this* close to hanging up on you."

"Cassie told me to call. Find out what we needed to bring to the cabin."

"I thought the girls got all of that squared away when Georgie threw that planning dinner last month?"

"Yeah, about that…Cass's attention was half-assed at best. We had a bet going, and…" Thatch paused and chuckled into the receiver. "Honestly, I never should have doubted my wife and her bag o' dick jokes. She must've texted no less than fifty to me that night."

Thatch, Cass, and ridiculous bets over dick jokes…
Did any of this surprise you?
It really shouldn't by now.

My eyebrows drew together. "Okay…so why doesn't she just call Georgie?"

"Something about the danger zone and Georgia being in her most fragile state. I don't know, bro. Why do I love titties so much? Just the way of the world."

I shook my head as I pulled into the underground garage at the office and parked in my spot. "Then, I guess, nothing. Georgia's got a list a mile long. I'd say you could call and offer to handle a couple of items on it, but I'm pretty sure she's attached to each and every item on a personal level."

"Like, how attached?"

"How attached are you to your nuts?"

"Wow. True love, then."

Despite the ridiculousness of the conversation, I chuckled. "I'd say so."

"How you handling all that focus, bro?"

"I'm good. She just wants it to be perfect, and I want her to be happy."

"All right. Let me know if I can help. Drop off a couple of extra kids for you to watch, that kind of thing."

"Thatch, I'm not watching your kids so you and Cassie can bang in the living room."

"Hah," he scoffed. "Kitchen's where it's at, son."

I laughed and shut off the car. "I'm at the office. Gotta go."

"Working? Oh yeah, heard that. I work for the money too. It's—"

I didn't even feel bad as I pushed the button to end the call. I'd have a whole Christmas of Thatch, thanks to my wife's plans, and I reckoned that was just about enough.

CHAPTER 3

All I Want for Christmas Is ~~You~~ Fluffing Perfection

Georgia

December 18th Afternoon

As I typed out an email to our Finance Department, my phone vibrated across my desk. I glanced down and sighed heavily.

Incoming call: Dr. Crazypants

Now that I'd let my mom know—via email, this morning, about an hour and a half ago—we wouldn't be celebrating Christmas with my family on Christmas Day, but instead, would be celebrating it together the week after, I'd been dodging her calls.

The red dot on the little phone on the left-hand bottom of my screen read ten—they were all from her.

Just woman up and answer it.

With a deep breath, I grabbed my phone and put it to my ear. Then I realized my body had protested the idea that I should answer all on its own and declined to hit the accept button. I quickly pulled the phone away, told my body to stop being such a pussy, and rectified my mistake before putting it back to my ear.

"Hey, Mom," I greeted in the happiest voice I could manage at noon on a workday.

"Hi, honey. Your father and I are both on," she responded, and my father chimed in, "Hi, Georgie girl."

Uh-oh...They're using the double-team tactic...

Their voices were too cheery, and my spidey senses immediately signaled *Danger! Danger!* Dick and Savannah only utilized the double-team tactic when their motivations revolved around getting what they wanted. Right now? They wanted Christmas together. I'd bet my blueberry crumble muffin on it—and I was really fucking hungry.

Stay strong, Georgia. Stay fucking strong.

"Hey, Dad," I said, and I swallowed hard against the awkward ball that had appeared inside my throat. "What are you guys up to today?"

"Well," my mother began, "we are getting our shopping list together and need to know what the girls want for Christmas."

I waited a few extra seconds for the rest of her spiel. I knew that had to be just the beginning, and the begging, pleading, guilt-tripping—bribing—had to be coming soon.

But, surprisingly, the line stayed silent.

"Georgie?" my dad asked. "You still there?"

My brows drew together in suspicion. What the hell was going on here? "Sorry...I got distracted by..." I searched my office for something to use as an excuse. "Jockstraps," I nearly shouted as my eyes landed on a poster of the current Mavericks team.

Jesus Christ. Jockstraps?

I squeezed my eyes tight and banged my head against the desk.

You're fucking ridiculous, Georgia.

My mom's voice was enthusiastic. "I can definitely see why

that'd be distracting."

Cripes.

"You got jocks in your office, George? You doin' inventory or somethin'?"

"No. Just…never mind about the jockstraps."

"You're the one who brought it up," my dad grumbled.

I sighed and did my best to pretend the conversation hadn't even happened. "I have a list of possibilities for toys I can email you, along with the girls' clothes sizes. Does that work?"

"That'd be perfect," my mom said. "Thanks, sweetheart."

"No problem. Is there anything else you need?" I cringed and shut my eyes at the same time. Why the fuck did I ask that? *Just hang up, you idiot!*

"Nope," my dad answered.

What?

"So, we'll see you, Kline, and girls on the twenty-ninth, right?"

"Right," I answered and slowly opened my eyes in disbelief.

"We're looking forward to it," he said without any inkling of irritation. In fact, his tone was one hundred percent jolly. "Well, we've gotta head out and finish up our shopping. Love you, Georgie girl."

"Oh, okay…"

"Love you, sweetheart," my mom added, and then the phone clicked dead.

Hell's bells, what had just happened?

I stayed frozen in my office chair for a good thirty seconds and stared at the wall.

I was shocked, to say the least. Any other holiday I'd ever tried to skip had been met with stern rebuttals and Dick's *I'm not putting up with your shit* face. I hadn't been able to see his face on the call, but he hadn't sounded at all constipated—a telltale sign of frustration for Dick Cummings.

I guessed I should've just been thankful they weren't suffocating me with guilt.

But I couldn't deny it made me a little suspicious…

Maybe they have plans of their own? Maybe they know something I don't?

I shook off those crazy thoughts.

Only Kline and our friends knew about our Christmas plans, and they knew not to spill the beans. Seriously, I'd done everything but threaten lives to keep the secret from any and all uninvited guests—*aka my parents and the rest of my entire fucking family.* I'd seen enough familial air humping and emergency situations for this holiday season, thank you very much.

But the most important thing right now wasn't paranoia or finding spots for my friends with the fishes. It was the fact that I only had seven days until Christmas, and just a few days until we'd leave for the Catskills.

The holiday countdown was *on*.

My to-do list was a mile long, and I had to get most of it done before the two-hour drive to our cabin in the mountains. Not to mention, with three more Mavericks' endorsement meetings scheduled this afternoon, and the rest of my workweek just as jam-packed, time wasn't on my side.

But come hell or high water, I'd get it done. I'd make sure this was the best Christmas Kline, my girls, or my friends had ever seen. I was determined to make this holiday flawless.

Perfect tree. Perfect decorations. Perfect food. Perfect. Perfect. *Perfect.* People would be Pinteresting our freakin' Christmas for years to come once I was through with it.

"Hey, Georgia," Winnie greeted as she walked into my office. "Wes said you just scored a huge endorsement deal this morning. Congrats, you little overachiever."

I shrugged. "All in a day's work, you know." If I was being

honest, it was one of the hardest deals I'd ever nailed down. Who knew a company that'd made its fortune off of sports drinks and energy bars could be so damn difficult?

She grinned and sat down in the seat across from my desk.

"But enough about the work chitchat," I redirected to the priorities. Million-dollar deals, schmeals, Christmas was number one on my list. "What time do you think you, Wes, and Lexi will get to the cabin on Christmas Eve?"

"We play at four on the twenty-third, so if everything goes smoothly, we'll be there early on Christmas Eve. Probably around ten."

"Man, I hope we win this one."

The Mavericks had two games left in the season, and this game, the one they'd play on the twenty-third, was a huge game. It would seal their spot in the play-offs and most likely ensure they only had to play one game to win the championship for their division.

"We will." Winnie winked.

"I dig the confidence, Win."

"Confidence is easy when our quarterback is in the best shape of his life."

Huge things were happening in the Mavericks organization, and if Quinn Bailey kept throwing touchdowns in the play-offs like he had been during the season, our team had a really good shot at winning *The Big Game*. The final game that decided who was the best team in the entire league.

Don't worry. I know it's called the Super Bowl. I'm not that sports-terminology challenged.

If we ended up pulling that off, scoring *more* million-dollar endorsement deals would be a piece of fucking cake for me.

"It also helps that my husband has a huge vested interest in the team," she teased. "It's pretty much Mavericks talk, all day, every day with Wes these days. I honestly have no idea how I managed to keep him focused enough to finish the rest of our Christmas shopping in the city last night."

"That you managed to get Wes to actually *do* the shopping is the part that amazes me," I admitted. Winnie was literally the only person on the planet who could get Wes Lancaster to engage in shopping—*holiday shopping*, at that. If that wasn't proof he worshiped the ground his wife walked on, I didn't know what was.

"Oh, by the way, you can send your presents with us if you want," I added. "Cass and I are going to wrap everything on the twenty-third while Kline and Thatch watch the kids." Well, none of them was actually aware of that plan, but minor details, right?

Needless to say, I had everything mapped out to a T.

Meals, décor, and exact times when everything would occur. This Christmas was going off with a jolly-fucking-bang that would be devoid of Meals on Wheels, *Twilight* arguments, and grill explosions.

I'm making this Christmas my holly jolly bitch.

"Wow," Win replied, relief evident in her voice and the tension release in her shoulders. "That would be fantastic if you guys could manage that, but I don't want to add any more to your plate… I know you've got a lot going on."

I waved her off with a nonchalant hand. "Oh, it's no problem." I mean, time wasn't on my side, but again, minor details. I didn't want any hiccups during this holiday, and the more things I had control over, the better.

Gratefulness kissed her lips in the form of a smile. "I'll have to make sure I text Cassie and tell her thank you."

"No need. I'll let her know." *After I let her know she is the one and only mandatory participant in my present-wrapping party…*

Win quirked a curious and far-too-knowing brow. "You haven't told her, have you?"

I shrugged and avoided eye contact like the plague. "Uh...I can't remember..."

"You can't remember?" she questioned on a laugh. "I call bullshit, Georgie."

"Fine," I said on a groan. "I'll call her now, and we can both tell her."

She grinned. "Fantastic."

Of course, Win just wanted to witness Cassie lose her shit over the idea of wrapping a million presents in one evening, but the call was much-needed. I had a bunch of other Christmas-related things to get finalized with Cass.

Plus, I had to make sure she and Thatch were all set for our car ride up to the Catskills. If there was one thing my best friend and her giant of a husband were good at it, it was running at least fifteen minutes behind schedule. And that was on a good day.

Their chronic tardiness was not going to put a hitch in my thoroughly planned and plotted Christmas itinerary. There was no way in Hades I was leaving my house any later than eight a.m. on the dot the morning we would head to the cabin. I had too many things to accomplish to be running even a minute behind schedule.

I grabbed my iPad off my desk and sat down beside Winnie. Two rings later and Cassie's pretty face was on my screen.

"Hey, ya floozies. Look at you two, rubbing tits together in the middle of the day. How's it hanging?"

Winnie and I laughed at our friend's colorful description but didn't address it. When it came to Cassie, it was almost always best to avoid falling further into her trap.

"Are you ready for the Catskills?" I asked, and Cass rolled her eyes.

"Good Lord, you're like a little Christmas Nazi, Wheorgie. But do not worry, my neurotic friend, the Kelly clan will be ready for the Catskills," she responded. "We still have a few more days until we leave."

"I'm not a Christmas Nazi," I refuted. I wasn't. I was the complete opposite, if you asked me. Everyone that was going to the cabin was about to have the best freakin' holiday of their lives. Hell, they'd be calling me Santa Claus before the festivities were through.

"You're a little over the top," she added. I settled for rolling my eyes rather than engaging in a verbal tug-of-war. I didn't have time for small, meaningless chitchat. This was a purely business conversation. The business being the best, most perfect Christmas that would ever occur.

"Anyway, I was calling to let you know you guys need to be ready to leave by seven."

"In the fluffing morning?" she questioned on a snort. "There is no way in hell I'm leaving at seven in the morning."

"Fine," I sighed. "Eight."

"How about nine?"

"No. Eight. I don't have time to waste, Cass."

"Fluffing hell, G. I've met drill sergeants who keep a looser schedule than you seem to have planned."

"We are going to have a perfect Christmas. *Perfect.* I refuse for it to be anything less."

Winnie cleared her throat, and I sighed.

"Also, you and I are going to wrap all of the presents on the twenty-third, which will fit into the schedule perfectly because—" I tried to sugarcoat the present-wrapping party, but Cassie cut me off before I could even spread the verbal icing.

"I hope by 'wrap,' you mean we're going to throw all of the shit into gift bags."

"Gift bags?" I gasped. Nightmarish visions of half-assed bags with crinkled-up tissue paper filled my head. "Hell *no*. There will be no gift bags. Everything will be wrapped. And don't worry, I bought the perfect paper and ribbon and bows for us to use."

Cass looked at Winnie. "Tell me you'll be joining us for the Christmas present sweatshop."

Win shrugged. "Sorry, Cass. We're not getting to the cabin until the next morning."

"Then let's reschedule Satan's wrapping marathon until then, Wheorgie."

"Nope," I responded immediately. "Christmas Eve is booked. We have breakfast at nine. Ice skating at ten. Hot cocoa and a Christmas movie at noon. Baking cookies for Santa at two—"

"Holy fluffing shit." Cassie cut me off. "Are you kidding me with this schedule right now?"

"Why would I joke about something like this?" I questioned in outrage. "This is Christmas we're talking about, Cassie!"

"Just take a breath, Mrs. Fluffing Claus," she muttered. "Everything will be fine."

"Everything will be fine if you stick to the schedule and wrap presents with me on the twenty-third."

"Fine. I'll wrap one million presents with you. Hell, I'll even ice-skate and bake cookies with Santa's balls on them, but you have to do something for me first."

"And what's that?"

"Convince Dean to watch Philmore."

"Seriously, Cassie?" I questioned. "It was hard enough to get him to stay at our house and watch Walter and Stan."

My fabulously gay best friend and old work husband nearly had a heart attack when I asked him to watch my giant dog and slightly persnickety cat. It'd actually taken an outrageously costly gift in the form of Prada shoes to get him to agree. How in the hell was I going to convince him to add another pet, a mini-pig, to be precise, to his pet-sitting duties? A new winter wardrobe courtesy of Versace?

Holy smokes, it was an expensive business to make Christmas perfect.

Don't tell, Kline.

"Take it or leave it, G."

I sighed. Once. Twice. Three times. Until finally, I came to the realization that I had no other option. "Fine."

"Perfect," she responded with glee shining in her eyes, and if the conversation had been in-person, I would've been real fucking tempted to smack her.

Once I'd ended the call and Winnie had left my office to head toward Wes's office to have a "chat" with the "boss," I pulled my Christmas agenda out of my purse and added yet another to-do item on page two of what felt like the never-ending list to achieve perfection.

Christmas To-Do's Cont'd
December 18th:
11. Organize the daily "Holiday Songs" playlist on iTunes.
12. Stocking stuffers for the kids.
13. Cookie decorations—sprinkles, ingredients for home-made icing (see page 15), chocolate, food coloring, marshmallows, Hershey Kisses, M&Ms.
14. Pick up and make copies of sheet music for Christmas Carols.
15. Fresh wreaths and garland will be ready for pick-up at the flower shop at 3 p.m.
16. Convince Dean to watch Philmore. (Preferably without an all-out catfight or expensive designer purchases.)

And this was just part of today's list.

Tomorrow's list made this one look like mere child's play.

It'd only taken a fifteen-minute subway ride and a four-minute walk, and I was inside the all-too-familiar offices of Brooks Media. After Win left, I'd rushed through my work so I could move on to the important stuff—Christmas—and the first thing on the list was Philmore.

Cassie had made it clear that her helping me with wrapping— one of the most important parts of the holiday—was contingent upon convincing Dean that pigs were cute and not just for bacon. Seeing as one of Dean's absolute favorite things was *meat*, I figured I had my work cut out for me.

Every time I stepped into this building, reminiscent memories of my days working for my husband hit me like a really warm wave. They were some of my fondest years, especially the one I'd spent falling in love with a man I'd held at arm's length for that long.

I missed working side by side with my favorite person on the planet, but I loved what I was doing at the Mavericks too. I had more room and freedom to spread my wings, and I never had to worry that my coworkers and peers were silently thinking my achievements were based on my relationship instead of my work ethic. With the Mavericks, it was all me. One hundred percent Georgia Brooks.

That still didn't stop my husband from trying to convince me to come back to work for him, but I didn't mind. It wasn't meant to be offensive; it was meant to be foreplay.

Believe me, it worked.

After a few hellos in the lobby to my favorite security men

and a short ride on the elevator, I was in the hub of one of the biggest cyberbusinesses in the country.

But I had a singular goal in mind today, so my heels click-clacked across the sleek, hardwood floors of the Brooks Media lobby without even a hello and went immediately in the direction of Dean's office.

Normally, I'd announce my plans for a visit, but in these circumstances, I felt that unexpected would only play in my favor. He'd have less time for interrogation.

"Knock, knock," I said as I rapped my knuckles on the half-opened door of Dean's office. "Got a minute to chat with an old friend?"

He looked up from his laptop, and a half-skeptical, half-happy look consumed his face. "Well, color me surprised. Come on in, little diva."

He watched me closely—*too closely*—as I made my way into his office and sat down in the chair across from his desk.

Just play it cool. Don't act like you're up to something.

"Hmmm…someone is being sneaky today, huh?"

Shit. I sat up straighter in the chair. *Act natural.*

"Not sneaky," I lied and forced a smile. "Just thought I'd stop in to say hello," I corrected, and Dean grinned.

"Uh-huh, sure. You just up and decided to take the fifteen-minute subway ride from your office to say *hello*. Makes complete sense."

"Are you calling me a liar?" I questioned, and he didn't miss a beat.

"That's exactly what I'm calling you."

"Sheesh, you're sassy today," I teased in my best attempt to keep him on the defense.

"Considering the fact that your husband still hasn't fired the she-devil Leslie, it's safe to say I'm a little on edge this afternoon…

every afternoon."

He had a point. Leslie had been the bane of my existence when I'd worked at Brooks Media. What she lacked in work ethic, she made up for in Instagram selfies and stealing people's food from the employee fridge. Needless to say, I was one hundred percent thrilled she was no longer a staple in my workday.

But I needed Dean to be more relaxed and less snarky and skeptical.

And there was only one certified way of getting Dean out of that kind of mood—compliments and fashion. Combine the two, and I'd be golden.

I glanced through the sleek and smooth glass of his desk and nodded toward his shoes. "At least your new Pradas look insanely hot."

"I know, right?" He wiggled his feet a little. "Not to mention," he started and made a show of tapping the collar of his shirt. "I also made a few purchases from the new Gucci winter line. This shirt is so gorgeous it should be preserved in a gilded frame and hung up in the freakin' Louvre."

"Right next to the *Mona Lisa*."

He winked. "You know it, girl."

"So, handsome good looks and amazing clothing aside…" I laid it on thick. "I wanted to give you a list of do's and don'ts for pet-sitting."

"Aha!" he exclaimed and pointed a perfectly manicured nail toward me. "So this visit was more *little Georgie is on the Christmas holiday warpath* instead of just a simple hello, huh?"

"It was both." I shrugged. "And I'm not on a Christmas holiday warpath. I'm spreading joy."

He grinned. "But it's okay if violence is needed to spread the joy, right?"

"Well, there *are* exceptions to every rule, Dean," I teased.

He chuckled and then waved his hand toward me. "All right, give it to me straight. Let me see what kind of neurotic, pet-sitting to-do list you've got for me."

"Who said I had a list?"

He quirked a perfectly plucked brow in my direction.

"Fine. I have a list. But I'm not neurotic. I'm just thorough."

Why did people keep calling me neurotic lately? I mean, just because I wanted everything perfectly planned out didn't make me a lunatic. I was merely meticulous and organized...*right?*

"Hand me the list of neuroses, little diva."

With only slight hesitation, I opened my purse and pulled out the sealed manila envelope that held everything Dean needed to know to watch Stan, Walter, *and* Philmore. Now, obviously, he knew about the first two, but I'd yet to enlighten him about the latest addition.

Hence, why the envelope was sealed. I was silently hoping he wouldn't open it until *after* I'd left his office...*and* we were already in the Catskills, too far for him to strangle me with his bare hands.

"Why is this thing taped up and glued shut like it holds the keys to Fort Knox?"

"I just wanted to make sure nothing fell out," I half lied. I mean, the keys and garage-door opener to our house were inside, so technically, I was sort of telling the truth.

"Well..." He set the envelope on his desk, and my shoulders sagged in relief. "I think I'll need some ibuprofen and glass of wine in order to read through this list without making me rethink my decision to watch your horse and evil gremlin while you guys go on some top-secret holiday vacation that you won't tell me about."

Normally, I wouldn't keep secrets from Dean. But I had to make sure no one found out where we were going. He had always been the office gossip, and God forbid, if he knew we were going to the Catskills, I had a feeling somehow my mother would find out. I was pretty sure the two of them still chatted occasionally.

"Dog and cat," I corrected. "Stan isn't that big, Dean, and Walter isn't evil. He's just particular."

He lifted a knowing brow in my direction.

"Fine," I relented. "I'll agree that Stan is nearly the size of a horse. But Walter is *not* evil. He's a total sweetheart once you get to know him."

Dean chuckled and shook his head. "I'm pretty sure you, Stan, and the girls are the only four living, breathing things that Walter is willing to tolerate. Everyone else is on his shit list for sure. Even Kline."

He was probably right, but that was beside the point. I needed to make him feel excited about watching the boys, not terrified.

"I promise, he'll be fine. Stan will keep him calm."

He pointed toward me. "I'm holding you to that, Georgie."

"Just make sure you read through everything so you know when to feed them." *And the fact that there will be three pets instead of two...* "What snacks you can give them, how much water to keep in their bowls, you know, just little stuff like that," I added.

"Just little stuff like that?"

"Uh-huh." I nodded and decided that since the envelope was still closed, now was the exact right time to get the hell out of his office. "All right," I said and stood up from my seat. "Thanks again for watching the boys. You're the best, Dean."

He just looked at me curiously as I offered a little goodbye wave.

"Well, I'll let you get back to it. See ya later and thanks again."

"Okay, little diva," he responded, but his eyes never left mine.

Yeah, I needed to get the hell out of his office and the Brooks Media building before he decided to open that envelope.

"Call me if you need anything," I added and did my best to

play it cool.

It took damn near all of my willpower not to sprint out the door. But somehow, I held it together, walking past the threshold of his office like a normal, sane person who wasn't trying to hide the fact that she'd just let one of her best friends know that he'd be watching a mini-pig along with a giant horse of a dog and a slightly evil cat in the absolute most cowardly way—via handwritten note.

But Dean was the biggest, baddest diva I'd ever met, and there was no doubt in my mind I'd fold like a fucking house of cards if he outright refused to watch Philmore.

The first inkling of guilt started to creep up my spine as I strolled down the hallway and toward the elevator, but a quick tug on my hand and my nearly tripping on my stilettos and falling face first onto the floor forced my focus elsewhere.

"Holy shit," I muttered, trying to control myself. But I didn't need to. Someone with the most familiar, sexy blue eyes I'd ever seen took control of my body for me. I couldn't stop my lips from quirking up into a smile.

"Hey, Benny," Kline whispered and led us toward a darkened corner of the hallway, far away from the ears and eyes of nosy employees.

I playfully tapped him on the chest. "You damn near scared the shit out of me, ya lunatic."

He just grinned. "What are you doing here?"

"I had to drop keys and pet instructions off to Dean."

He raised a questioning brow and wrapped his arms tighter around my waist. "And you weren't going to stop by your husband's office and say hello?"

"I have so many things on my to-do list, Kline," I whined. "I don't have a lot of time."

"Ouch." He feigned discomfort. "Couldn't even make a

little time for a short hello or hug or innocent little kiss for your husband?"

"I'm sorry." I placed a soft, tender kiss to his lips. "It wasn't personal, I promise. I just wanted to make sure I got everything done today."

He pouted. "It feels a little personal, Benny."

"It's not." I kissed his lips again, and he grinned. "I promise."

"You know what I think?"

"What do you think?"

"I think you should come into my office and make it up to me," he whispered slyly, and it took a whole lot of strength not to give in to his sexy demands.

"Nope," I responded immediately. "Not happening. Last time we did that, I got pregnant with Evie."

He winked. "Exactly. And she's perfect."

"We do not need another baby right now, Kline!" I exclaimed on a whisper. "Two kids and two pets means we're already outnumbered."

His smile made my knees feel weak.

I slid out of his arms and backed away from his too charming, outright devilish smile. "You stay right there," I instructed and pointed toward the floor his feet stood on. "And I'm going to go this way." I pointed behind me, in the direction of the elevator. "Far, far away from your crazy ideas right now."

"I love you," he whispered.

It was moments like this that made it damn near impossible not to swoon right out of my stilettos. "I love you too," I whispered back and walked toward the elevator doors. One hit for the down button and the cart dinged its arrival.

"Oh, and Benny?" Kline questioned as I stepped inside the elevator. He'd followed me to the doors and leaned casually inside.

"Yeah?"

"You and me—we're a power team. We'll never be outnumbered."

As he stepped out of the way and the elevator doors closed, I couldn't wipe the smile off my face.

My husband. He was too damn charming for my own good sometimes.

My smile stayed firmly in place as I tilted my head back to look at the floor numbers at the top of the elevator. Halfway down, my phone pinged with a text message. I rooted around in my purse and clicked to open it.

Dean: You owe me big-time, Pig Swindler.

Oh, shit. He'd opened the envelope…

I didn't even have time to respond. Another text came mere seconds later.

Dean: Big. Time.

The second text contained a link. To Christian Louboutin's website.

Thank God my husband is a billionaire…

I went ahead and clicked through on the link, figuring I was better off ordering Dean's payoff now. I had no doubt he'd be expecting payment by the time of delivery of the animals, and even expedited shipping took a day or two.

The elevator pinged to indicate my arrival on the bottom floor, and the doors made a distinct sound as they slid open. Without looking up, I stepped forward and off, and unfortunately, walked right into a human.

"Oh, sh—sorry," I said, stopping myself just before cursing at some stranger.

Warm hands circled my shoulders, and a familiar voice made me completely abandon the designer apparel search to look up.

"Kline," I gasped. "What are you doing down here?"

I looked at the elevator behind me and back again. "*How* are you down here?"

He leaned forward and touched his lips to mine, grabbed my hand, and started toward the front doors of the lobby immediately.

I hurried at double my normal pace to keep up, a thrill running through me at this completely unplanned turn of events.

"Kline!" I snapped, my frustration at being in the dark the only thing helping me maintain my ability to be snippy about anything. My adrenaline from the unexpected excitement had my body humming.

He glanced back at me as he held the front door open and ushered me through, explaining, "The service elevator is a little faster."

"Okay," I mumbled, my focus fixated on trying to keep up as he pulled my hand tight to his chest to keep my body close and weaved our way through the New York sidewalk traffic like a pro. "But why? Where are we going?"

My husband winked. Apparently, verbal explanations had become overrated.

Fortunately, he didn't maintain the mystery long, ducking into The Q, a hotel on the corner about a block up from Brooks Media. We went straight to the desk, where the clerk was waiting with a key in hand. My husband said nothing, and the clerk did nothing more than acknowledge, "Mr. Brooks," as he handed over the key.

I let out a strangled giggle as we moved away from the desk and headed straight for the elevator bank on the opposite wall. "You know, if you weren't the man you are to me, I'd be freaking the fluff out about your ability to walk in here and get a key without saying a word, like a freakin' regular."

Kline chuckled and pulled my hand at his chest up to his lips to kiss my knuckles softly. "I called on my way down at the office."

"Oh…" I muttered. "Okay."

Thank Jesus. But still…

"What are we doing?" I asked, in search of explanation once again. Kline dragged me into the elevator as it arrived, and the doors closed in front of us, closing us in on our own.

Still mindful of the cameras, I'm sure, Kline leaned down, the skin of his perfect lips skimming the shell of my ear, and whispered his answer. "We're going to fuck."

I blinked, and then, as soon as my body registered his words, clenched my thighs together to conceal the rush of wetness between my legs.

"Oh my God."

"Raw. Hard. Sweet and fucking soft," he whispered on. "Whatever you want. Just as long as I get to spend an hour in that perfect pussy of yours."

"Sweet, sweet Jesus," I chanted.

I could feel myself spasming between my legs from just his words. Suddenly, it seemed like a really fucking good idea to go off schedule for a little while.

The elevator doors finally opened, and Kline chuckled as *I* dragged *him* down the hall. Unfortunately, in my excitement, I'd forgotten I had no fucking clue what room we were in, and he had to pull me to a stop and change our direction.

"This way, baby," he said, smiling widely. "I really love your enthusiasm, though."

I blushed a little as we stopped in front of a room, and he set about unlocking it. The door clicked open, and he held it as I stepped through.

I started to look around, at the expensive white curtains, the chaise settee in the corner, and the fluffy cream duvet on the bed, but it all disappeared as the door fell shut with a slam and my husband's adoring hands fell on me.

"Kline," I whispered as his lips went to work on my neck, pulling the skin inside and nipping it with his teeth every so often. I tugged at my coat, but he was already divesting me of it, throwing it blindly at a chair behind him and then going back instantly to the buttons on the front of my blouse.

"Hottest woman I've ever seen in my life, baby." His hands skimmed my body and around my hips to cup my ass. "You get me hard every goddamn time I see you."

His hands came back to my last two buttons and made short work of them as he pressed his hands into my ass to prove it.

I moaned.

He pulled my opened shirt from my shoulders and unhooked my bra, so I helped him by pulling it down my arms and tossing it away. I heard fabric ripping, and then the heat of his bare skin hit my back.

"Holy shit," I gasped, his hands fondling my breasts and rolling my nipples. "Did you just rip your shirt off?"

He spun me fast, and I teetered, but he steadied me at my hips and then lifted. I shrieked and grabbed at his shoulders as he walked me back to the bed and dropped me onto my back with a plop.

"Told you, baby," he said with a grin. "I'm gonna fuck you, and I'm gonna do it for at least an hour. I'm not wasting time on my shirt."

"You unbuttoned mine," I pointed out.

He smiled and leaned down to circle my nipple with his tongue. Against my skin, he explained, "You care about yours."

"Kline—"

"Quiet, baby," he ordered as he pulled my skirt and panties

down over my hips and tossed them away. "I'm busy."

My eyes narrowed for the briefest hint of second…until his mouth closed over my clit and sucked.

Ho-ly shit.

His eyes burned as he watched me watch him. He worked me slow at first—just teasing me with his tongue with soft flicks and long licks—but as I started to moan, my blood pumping a blush into the skin all over my body, he upped his pace and intensity until I hovered at the peak.

My eyes closed and rolled, my back arching involuntarily as his hands squeezed at my hips roughly, and he hummed.

I started to fall, but he didn't wait for me to finish, climbing up onto the bed, covering me with his body, and slamming inside. I wasn't sure when he'd gotten his pants off, and I didn't fucking care. All I needed was my husband's enraptured face as he seated himself inside me.

Him and me? *We* were *perfect.*

CHAPTER 4

~~Jingle~~ Hell's Bells

Kline

December 22nd

Thirty minutes into our car ride and Georgia was finally starting to get over the fact that Cassie and Thatch hadn't followed through with their plans to ride with us.

Normally, I might have gloated that I'd known they wouldn't be riding with us the moment she'd decreed we were leaving at eight a.m., but under these circumstances, with my wife this tense, I thought better of it.

Instead, I'd spent the time reminiscing over the moments where the view of the open road that led to an exciting destination was fun—adventurous, even.

That was before kids. Way, way before kids.

Forty-five minutes into our car ride and the famous golden arches that signified grease, burgers, and fries were a welcomed sight for not only Julia, but me too.

And an hour into our car ride, I was thankful for full bellies and iPads.

This, my friends, was life with kids.

When we were at home, my wife and I strived to feed our girls healthy meals void of fast food and high-fructose corn syrup. We also did our best to keep them active versus sitting around staring at the television or an electronic device all day long.

But in the car, with a fussy eighteen-month-old and an outspoken and cranky five-year-old, we only cared about keeping the peace. If a Happy Meal and *My Little Pony* on Netflix was the solution, then by God, we accepted it with open fucking arms.

First lesson of parenthood: Pick your battles.

Second lesson of parenthood: Take everyone else's lessons and tell them to fuck off. What works for one kid doesn't necessarily work for another. Do what works for you.

Right now, as we headed up Route 17, headphones, iPads, and French fries were working for me.

The car was joyously free of whining and tears, and only the soft sounds of Frank Sinatra serenading us with holiday tunes filled my ears.

Thank everything.

"Are you ready to enjoy a quiet Christmas at the cabin, baby?" I asked and reached out and patted my beautiful wife's thigh.

"You have no idea how ready I am." Georgia smiled, and then after a few blissfully quiet moments, she pulled her planner out of her purse.

Oh God. Not the planner...

With a flip of her wrist, she opened it to her bookmarked page. "There is so much to do, Kline. The second we get to the cabin, we need to get unpacked, get the tree, decorate the house with lights—"

I'd been doing everything in my power to stay one step ahead of my wife with this holiday schedule of hers. She wanted a perfect Christmas with her family and friends, but I feared she was going to drive herself literally crazy trying to control and plot out every detail.

She meant well. I knew she meant well. Hell, after spending several holidays with her family, and watching shit hit the fan every single time, I understood her need for a flawless holiday. But holy shit, I feared my Georgie was near the brink of imploding.

And it's really hard to fuck a collapsed bucket of mush. I hadn't tried, but I was a man and I could visualize. Not nearly as appealing as my wife in her current state.

She didn't even realize she was going over the top with this, so I saw it as my responsibility to make sure she didn't step too far over the line.

Again with the imploding and lack of fucking, etc.

"The tree and lights are already taken care of, Benny."

"What?" Her eyes went wide with surprise. "What do you mean, they've already been taken care of?"

"I hired someone to hang the lights for us. They'll be at the cabin around noon, and all you need to do is tell them where and how many."

Now, I'd never been a fan of wasting money on things I could do myself, but when it came to my wife's sanity—and my own—I didn't give a shit about the cost.

"I'm really happy about the lights, but what about the tree?" she asked. "Tell me you didn't just have some random person pick out our Christmas tree, Kline. It's tradition that we—"

"Don't worry. We'll be picking out our tree," I corrected. "I contacted the owner of the tree farm you fell in love with when we bought the cabin. All we need to do is pick the tree out *ourselves*," I added with a smirk, "and he has someone ready to deliver it and set it up for us."

"Wow. Kline. I…" Georgia looked over at me. Eyes wide. Mouth slightly parted in a little "o."

Speechless.

Fuck yeah. One win for me.

I placed my hand on her thigh and squeezed gently. "We're a team, Benny."

She smiled and a few moments later, whispered, "Thank you."

Little did she know, that gorgeous smile of hers was the only thanks I needed.

Happy wife. Happy life.

When we made it to the cabin, the girls took off for their room, Julia patiently helping Evie up the stairs, and Georgie went right to work.

Instead of trying to redirect her to relaxing, loosening up, or something that was more enjoyable than closely studying her to-do list, I took the opportunity to head out back and get some firewood chopped for the next few days without interruption.

Georgia usually teased me that I liked to do it myself, with an old-fashioned ax rather than a wood splitter, no less, but it never changed my mind.

Something about the repetitiveness, simplicity, and physical exertion of splitting logs by hand cleared my mind and settled my soul.

This was life. This was love. This was me providing for my family in a way my relatives used to before life got so complicated.

Once I started, though, I was fully involved. So it was actually a surprise when Georgia came out a couple of hours later to tell me that Thatch and Cassie and their kids, Ace and Gunner, had arrived.

I wiped some sweat off of my forehead with the back of my arm and smiled at the look in my wife's eyes. She might tease me about chopping wood, but it turned her on tremendously.

"Okay, baby. I'll come in and take a quick shower. Then we can get busy on your activities list."

All of the arousal swimming in her eyes doubled in volume.

Who knew Christmas talk was the way to go?

I almost laughed as she bit her lip and shifted to squeeze her legs together.

"Cass is already protesting organized activity."

She was still smiling, which was eerie given her words. I couldn't help but question it.

"That doesn't upset you?"

She winked and clapped her hands together with glee. "I'd already built in five hours of settling time while I sorted the lights—which you already did—so I just made up a bunch of stuff so she'll be more amenable later when I really want to do things. Right now, she thinks she's getting one over on me."

"Quite cunning, Mrs. Brooks," I congratulated.

"Well, thank you, Mr. Brooks," she accepted with a jump, twist, and kick of her foot as she headed back to the house.

I quickly stacked the smattering of logs I'd just split and followed her in.

The shower was hot and glorious, and the only thing that would have made it better was some company from my wife. But I knew better than to expect her to pop in when she had four kids and Cassie and Thatch downstairs to keep her occupied.

I got dressed quickly in a pair of jeans and a long-sleeved T-shirt and trotted down the stairs to the sound of Thatch's booming voice.

He was even more animated than normal, and it drew me straight to the kitchen like a magnet, out of curiosity to find out what had him so fired up.

When I got there, I found him with his ass on my counter, long legs hanging nearly to the floor, and Georgia and Cassie were looking on as he talked at his phone to someone on FaceTime.

"Tell me Mitchell's hamstring isn't acting up!"

Ah, Wes.

Wes's answering voice was annoyed. "Stop making up injuries, for Christ's sake. Mitchell is fine, Sean is fine, Bailey is fine, the whole team is fucking fine. But I swear on the perkiness of Cassie's tits, you won't be fine if you keep trying to jinx us."

Thatch's face darkened. "You can't threaten my wife's tits! That's a personal foul, asshole."

"Hmm," Wes muttered, unfazed. "I can, and I did. Flat, saggy, meatless tits. That's all you'll have to play with for the rest of your life if you don't cool it."

Thatch's face turned panicked as he looked to Cassie to confirm the curse hadn't already set in. She squeezed them together and let them bounce before rolling her eyes. "Perky and full, Thatcher. Relax."

Georgia charged though, using the opportunity to snag the phone from his hand.

"Wes—"

"Hi, Georgia," he greeted.

She waved a hand in front of her face and scrunched her nose. "Yeah, yeah, hi. Can you put Winnie on?"

Quite frankly, I didn't even think any of them had noticed I was in the room yet.

Wes sighed but passed the phone. I could hear Winnie's laugh as she took it. "Hey, Georgie!"

"Hi! I've got a list for you so you can tell Lex what to expect. Do you have a pen?"

Lex, Winnie and Wes's daughter, was high-functioning on the

autism spectrum. Schedule, planning, and advanced notice were comforts for her, and with one simple comment, Georgia made it clear—even with a brain full of chaos—she had a mind to that.

Thatch and Cassie glanced to me, and all at once, all of us fell more in love with my wife.

This was why we were here.

This was what kept us coming back for more.

This was what made me one of the luckiest guys alive.

CHAPTER 5

Please ~~Come~~ Go Home for Christmas

Georgia

December 23rd

Only one alarm and zero snooze buttons, and I was up and out of the bed before my husband. Consider it a record and the complete opposite of the norm. Kline was much better at being on time, always waking up at seven on the dot every morning, and I had a long-standing track record of running fifteen minutes behind.

But not today, people. Not freakin' today.

I had too many thoughts of Christmas to-do's swirling about in my holiday-fueled brain.

"What time is it?" Kline asked, his voice all raspy and sleep-filled. Goodness, he sounded sexy. I had the urge to crawl back into bed with him.

Stay strong, Georgia! Do not give in to temptation.

"It's half past seven," I answered, but I also kept my holiday game face on. Instead of losing precious planning time worshiping my husband's naked body—*don't worry, I'll make up for it tonight*—I slipped on a pair of jeans, a thermal shirt, and my favorite cream sweater. If this outfit didn't scream rustic cabin and happy holidays, I didn't know what would.

I know. I know…You probably think I'm going slightly overboard with this, but I honestly think anyone who has had to experience a lifetime of tragic holiday celebrations with my family would do the same.
One Christmas, Aunt Rhonda called Blanche Devereaux a floozy whore who never should have been allowed to be a character on The Golden Girls, *and I had to tamp down the urge to rage just so I could hold back my mother.*

"Baby, it's too early." A soft, tired groan left his lips as he turned onto his back and patted the empty spot beside him. "The sun is barely up. Come back to bed."

"Nope," I responded, sitting down on the chaise lounger and slipping on my coziest and cutest pair of gray boots. "There is too much to do, which means I have no time to waste."

"Benny," Kline taunted. "Everyone is still asleep," he said, and his voice had dropped to a deep and seductive tone. "I promise you there will be no wasting of time in this bed."

Oh, Lord. Please give me strength, I silently prayed. Surely, Jesus would understand my dilemma. It was *His* birthday I was trying to make perfect.

"Baby, come back to bed," he repeated, and my knees started to buckle.

Oh no… Don't look at him. Don't even make eye contact with him.

I closed my eyes and said, "No, Kline. I have too many things to get done today."

"Well, at least come over here and give your husband a kiss."

I opened my eyes and blew him a kiss from the doorway, and he smirked.

With his blues glimmering and his hair all tousled and sexy, my husband was too tempting for my own good, and a real kiss was too persuasive on the wrong side of the battle with my vagina.

But my husband wasn't taking my shit, floozy, temptress vagina or not.

"Not good enough," he stated and sat up in the bed, his bare and toned torso peeking above the white comforter. "A real kiss, Benny girl." He made a little come-hither motion with his index finger.

"One kiss." I put a defiant hand to my hip. "One kiss and no monkey business. Got it?"

He grinned. "Got it."

I strode with purpose, closing the distance between us, and the instant I leaned down to give him a gentle yet very PG kiss to his lips, he snagged his arms around my waist and yanked me back into bed with him.

"Kline!"

He chuckled and flipped me onto my back, maneuvering his strong frame above mine. "God, you're beautiful."

Shit.

He kissed my neck, and my body betrayed me, a moan slipping past my lips.

Double shit.

"Kline," I half whined and half moaned when his greedy lips moved across my neck and up to my ear. "I don't have time for distractions."

"I thought I was your husband." His quiet, amused chuckles pushed warm air against my skin. "Not a distraction."

"Right now, you're both *and* one hundred percent evil."

He leaned back, and his blue eyes met mine. "I'm just a man who is crazy in love with his beautiful wife."

This man would be the death of me. One day, I'd swoon myself straight into a fluffing coma.

"You're truly the sweetest, most perfect man I know, and I love you deeply," I said and touched his cheek. "But right now, I can't let you unleash that swoony charm of yours on me. I have one million things to accomplish before this day is done."

He quirked an adorable brow. "Swoony charm?"

"Oh, don't act all naïve and innocent."

My husband smirked and pressed a soft, tender kiss to my lips. "Okay, I will let you off this bed, but only under one condition," he said. And then added, "Actually, make that two conditions."

"And what would those conditions be?"

"Put on a pot of fresh coffee, *and* promise me that tonight, after we put the kids to bed, I get to distract you in this bed as much as I fucking want."

"Deal." I pressed a smacking kiss to his lips. "Now let me go so I can get a move on it."

"You got it," he whispered, and after a playful slap to my ass, he let me on my determined way.

After a quick peek into the girls' bedroom to find them still sound asleep, I headed downstairs to the kitchen. I smiled to myself when only the gorgeous sounds of silence filled my ears. Everyone else was still in bed, and I could ease into my day without chaos. I was damn near giddy over the thought.

Once I preheated the oven for today's breakfast of cinnamon rolls and filled up the coffee machine with fresh water and set it to brew, I sat down on one of the wooden kitchen barstools and started to peruse this morning's agenda.

Christmas To-Do's

December 23rd:

1. *Laundry: Wash the adults' and kids' pajamas for Christmas Eve.*

2. *9:00 a.m.: Cinnamon Roll Breakfast.*

3. *10:00 a.m.: Grocery store for fresh items for Christmas Eve dinner and Christmas Day breakfast and dinner.*

4. *12:00 p.m.: Make Your Own Pizza lunch with the kids.*

5: *1:00 p.m.: Make (and wrap) the dads' Christmas gifts from the kids.*

5. *2:00 p.m.: Christmas Story Time with Santa Thatch.*

6. *3:00 p.m.: Wrap presents with Cassie.*

The coffee machine dinged its gorgeous alarm, and I glanced away from my agenda and focused on the first order of business for today: coffee. Once my veins had reached their daily caffeine quota and breakfast was in the oven, I could dive headfirst into today's planned events.

I hopped off my barstool and grabbed a Santa-themed mug from the cabinet, and moments later, my taste buds danced over that first sip of fresh brew.

There really was nothing like that initial sip of coffee in the morning. Pure heaven, I tell you.

With my mug in hand, I took in the cabin's wooded views while I finished the morning's first cup of coffee. Slightly distorted snow-capped mountains and evergreen trees told me that seeing everything from the window wasn't enough. I wanted to feel the crisp temperature against my skin and inhale the fresh mountain air, and I wanted the edges of nature's beauty to be stark and defined.

After tossing on my jacket and scarf, I headed out onto the back deck. Between the peace and quiet and the breathtaking sights, it was better than I'd remembered. This view was exactly why Kline and I had decided to purchase this rustic cabin.

Gosh, I love this place.

I grinned to myself and lifted my mug to take another sip of coffee, but my hand paused in midair when I heard a faint, *"Come out here!"* coming from somewhere behind me.

What the heck? I swear that sounds exactly like my dad...

My eyes went wide for a beat until I realized it would be absolutely ridiculous and impossible for my parents to be anywhere near our cabin. They knew nothing of our plans nor our location, and they'd never been up to our cabin before now.

I laughed to myself as I shook off the absurdity of my thoughts. They weren't here. *I'm imagining it.*

"Dick!" a different, still very familiar voice called, only louder this time. "Where are you?"

"I'm outside! Come check out this view, Vanna! You're going to love it!"

What in the ever-loving shit? Fuck, fuck, fluffing fuck.

I strode across the deck and headed for the porch. Coffee sloshed out of my mug with every other step, but I didn't care. I had to see if what I was hearing was real.

I rounded on the cabin, my heart beating very nearly out of my chest, and I peeked around the final corner with fear filling my whole body from bottom to top.

A giant RV occupied every square inch of our front yard.

Like, literally every square fucking inch.

Not to mention, my father, Dick Cummings, stood outside the RV's door in a red velvet bathrobe, bare legs covered only by a pair of black galoshes, and a giant smile consuming his face.

"Georgie!" he called toward me. "We made it!"

My jaw didn't hit the ground; I was pretty sure it just fell right off my fucking face.

"Dick!" my mother shouted as she opened the RV door. "Oh! There you are!"

"Look who's awake, Vanna," my dad announced as he pointed toward me. "Our favorite Georgie girl!"

My mother looked across the yard to find me standing slack-jawed and most likely one skipped heartbeat away from passing the fuck out. "Oh, Georgie honey! Good morning!"

"We burned the midnight oil getting here last night!" my dad exclaimed. "But have no fear, we managed to get a few hours of shut-eye so we can join in on all the holiday fun today!"

Have no fear? Was he fucking kidding me?

Fear was the *only* emotion I had.

Visions of Christmases past danced around in my head, and by the time my thoughts had rounded Terror Lane and headed straight for Worst-Case Scenario Boulevard, I had to shut my eyes just to avoid the possibilities of what another holiday spent with my parents would mean. Explosions…the cabin going up in flames…the deck sliding down the mountain…

And the insurance policy on this cabin was in *my* name! At least disaster at their house didn't up my premiums.

"What in the fluffing hell is going on? It's not even nine in the morning!" my best friend's voice filled my ears, and I opened my eyes to find her peeking outside the French doors of one of the guest bedrooms.

"Cass! Who's out there?" Thatch's voice filled the otherwise quiet morning air, and moments later, his giant head peeked over Cassie's shoulder and out the doors. "What the hell is that?" He squinted against the early morning sun. "Who parked their house on the lawn?"

"Cass! Thatch!" my mother called up toward them with a wave. "Good morning!"

"Savannah?" Cassie questioned, and my father went ahead

and answered for her.

"It's Dick and Savannah, honey!"

Both Cassie and Thatch grinned. Like actual, happy grins.

Those were two things I wasn't feeling or doing in that moment. Hadn't anyone remembered the point of this holiday was to avoid the tragic Christmas scenarios that stuck to my family like glue?

"Dick, my man," Thatch hollered down at my parents. "When did you get here?"

"Late last night!"

"That's fantastic!"

It only took a few moments of shouting for my body to eventually jolt out of its frozen state of shock. "All right! Everyone inside. We don't need the neighbors to think there's some sort of domestic dispute."

"Sorry, Georgie!" my dad continued to shout, and I cringed. "We'll get dressed and come inside for breakfast! Hope you're making something good for us!"

Jesus Christ. Making something good for *them*? I didn't even fucking invite them.

But seriously, who *did* invite them? That was the biggest question of the morning.

I looked up at Cassie and Thatch and scrutinized their faces. Was it them? Were they the assholes who spilled the beans to my parents?

Eventually, Cassie's eyes met mine, and she immediately started shaking her head. "It wasn't me, Wheorgie," she called down. "It was *not* me."

"What wasn't you, Cassie?" my mother yelled toward her.

"I was just telling Georgia that all of the loud sex groans last night were from Thatcher," she lied. "He gets so horned up when I tickle his balls while we're banging."

Yeah, real nice cover-up, Cass.

Nothing said Happy Holidays like a good old testicle tickle.

I shut my eyes and sighed.

If anyone ever wanted to know what *The Nightmare Before Christmas* really looked like, it was this—my best friend shouting about tickling her husband's balls while my dad scratched his own through his Hugh Hefner-style robe on my front lawn.

"Hey, Thatch, check this out!" My dad's voice forced me to open my eyes again. "Merry Christmas! Shitter was full!" he exclaimed as he reenacted the infamous scene from *Christmas Vacation* with a hose from our yard pointed directly toward the sewer.

Thatch and my dad started cracking up, and I wanted to kill everyone.

"Dad!" I called his attention. "Get dressed and meet me in the kitchen. I've got cinnamon rolls and coffee for breakfast."

He responded with a thumbs-up and a smile, and I headed inside before I did or said something I would regret.

As I walked into the kitchen and put the cinnamon rolls in the oven, I mentally added another item to my to-do list.

ASAP: Figure out who in the fuck invited my parents to Christmas in the Catskills.

CHAPTER 6

~~Feliz~~ Fu-luffing Navidad

Kline

December 23rd Afternoon

"Vanna!" Dick shouted from the entryway as he slipped on his boots and opened the front door. "It's time, sweet cheeks! Come to the RV and give Dick some sugar!"

I could hear Georgia's sigh from the kitchen as she worked on a chocolate cream pie for tonight's dessert.

Her mother giggled. "Just a few minutes, honey! I'm just finishing up this eggnog, and I'll meet you there!"

"I'll be the strapping man in his birthday suit sprawled out on our bed!" Dick called over his shoulder before stepping onto the front porch and shutting the door behind him.

"It's Papas birthdays, Daddy?" Julia asked me with wide, excited eyes. "I wants a birthdays suit for mines birthdays too!"

I glanced toward the kitchen, and by the look on my wife's face—exasperation, annoyance, *at the end of her fucking rope*—I knew she'd had more than her fill of her parents. They'd been here, inside the cabin, trying to take charge of everything Georgie had planned for the day since this morning.

My wife's cinnamon roll breakfast? Dick had to add pancakes, eggs, and bacon.

The two p.m. Christmas book with the kids? What had started out as Thatch reading *The Polar Express* had turned into Dick showing the kids funny YouTube videos of dogs dressed up as elves.

Pretty much everything my wife had planned, her parents had decided to put their own twist on it. Hell, the fact that she'd lasted a whole seven hours without strangling one of them was a Christmas miracle.

"Papa is just being funny," I responded. "It's not really his birthday."

"But whys he gonna wears his birthdays suit?"

Thanks a lot, Dick.

"It's probably just a funny suit that makes Mimi laugh a lot."

"Can I's sees it? I like funny things!"

Unless you want to be traumatized for the rest of your life…

"No, sweetheart," I responded and quickly utilized the redirection tactic. "Guess what?"

"What?"

I kneeled down and whispered into her ear, "I know where Mommy hid the special Christmas candy."

Julia grinned from ear to ear.

"But you have to promise to keep it a secret."

"I promises! I promises!" she exclaimed on a whisper-yell. "Can I haves some now?"

"I promise when Mommy is busy with something upstairs, I'll sneak you a piece," I said quietly. "But you have to promise to keep it a secret. Deal?"

"Deals, Daddy." She nodded and held out her little hand to seal it. "I won't tells anyone. Not even Ace."

"Good girl." I smiled. "Now, go find Ace and see what Christmas movie he wants to watch later."

"Okay!" she shouted and ran for the hallway just as Georgie gave me the secret signal that she'd be sneaking upstairs to one of the spare bedrooms to get everything ready to wrap presents.

Yeah. My wife even had secret signals planned out. Ones that I was required to memorize, mind you.

Good thing she was so fucking adorable.

"Dude!" Thatch's booming voice echoed from the living room. "Get back in here! The third quarter just started!"

I glanced at my watch and realized the Mavericks had probably started playing the second half five minutes ago, and I made my way toward the TV. Thatch was sprawled out on a leather recliner.

"Bailey looks like he's ready to kick some serious tail."

I grinned. "If he plays as well as he did the first half, I think we can pull this one out."

"Kline!" my mother-in-law called from the kitchen. "Let Georgie know I'll be back later, but I left my eggnog in the fridge for her and Cassie!"

I nodded. "Will do."

Thirty minutes later, and Thatch and I were one hundred percent invested in the game. Well, we *were*, until Cassie walked in while corralling all four kids into the living room with us.

"Listen up, boys," she instructed.

Both Ace and Gunner turned to listen, but she shook her head. "No babies, Mommy's talking to the big boys right now."

Thatch reached out a hand instead of turning his attention away from the TV and felt blindly for his wife. Unsurprisingly, his hand made contact with her boob, and he proceeded to honk it.

She smacked his hand and then went for his dick, and he did a bob and weave to the side.

I smirked and suggested with a chuckle, "Maybe Wes should bring you on as a contractor to work on the players' moves."

"I got reflexes, son," Thatch commented back automatically.

"Men!" Cassie snapped. "Take your chickens out of your hands long enough to fluffing listen to me."

"Chickens in hands, chickens in hands," Ace chanted.

"Chickens?" I questioned, and Thatch turned hard eyes to me.

"Yeah, Kline. Chickens. The old chicken fight. Chicken-a-doodle-doo."

"I think I got it," I said with a smirk before taking a pull of my beer. "Our Richards."

"Exactly," Cassie confirmed. "I know they're both big—" She leaned around Thatch and made eyes at me, whispering low enough so little ears couldn't hear, "Especially yours, Big-dick Brooks."

I smiled, and Thatch snapped, "Hey!"

"But you have an assignment. You are on kid duty until further notice."

Thatch jerked his head to the TV with a whine. "But the game's onnnnn."

"Listen," Cassie whispered menacingly. "If I have to go up there and slap paper into the shape of swans with the Christmas Monster, you have to watch the kids. Deal with it."

Thatch opened his mouth to whine some more, but I cut in. "That's fine, Cass. Go on up and have fun."

"Yeah, fun," she remarked with a scoff. "That and pulling my hair out by the roots. My two favorite activities."

Thatch swung an arm around her shoulders and nuzzled his big head into her neck. Unfortunately, that didn't mean his next words were too low for me to hear. "Oh, come on. You know you like a little hair-pulling."

Christ.

"Bye, Cassie," I called, and they thankfully broke it up. She gave me a thumbs-up as she was leaving, and Thatcher broke down into a near fit of giggles.

"What in the h-e-double hockey sticks is so funny?"

He jerked his head to the door and smiled. "That's her new PG way of giving the finger."

The crowd on the TV got loud suddenly, and both of us turned to the screen to find out the cause—PG middle finger completely forgotten.

Fourth quarter, eighteen seconds on the clock, third down, and the Mavericks had the ball. Shit had just gotten real.

"Fu-luffing hell. Bailey needs to convert this pass, or else Miami is going to ruin their shot at a bye during the division play-offs."

"Fuluffing?" I repeated with a grin. "That's a new one."

"Suck it, K," Thatch muttered, but not quietly enough for his mini-me.

"Suck it!" Ace shouted gleefully and punctuated his words with two finger guns firing in the air. "Suck it! Suck it!"

"Listen, little dude..." Thatch sighed and stopped his son with a gentle grab of his wrist, midair gun shootout. "Do not repeat anything I say for the next five minutes. Not a single word, understand?"

The next five minutes? How about the rest of his life? That would've been a better approach in my humble opinion.

"Yeah, I guess." Ace shrugged. "But after five minutes, no big deal?"

I chuckled, and Thatch flashed a glare in my direction.

"How about just don't repeat anything I say, okay?"

"O-kaaaaay, Daddio," he responded with a little nod and then sprinted toward the kitchen where Julia was sitting at the table watching *My Little Pony* on her iPad. "Lia! My dad says we can't say suck it no more!"

"What's suck it?" my daughter asked, and I sighed.

"I don't know," Ace responded. "But I like saying it."

Of course he loved saying it. He was Thatch's son.

"What's sucks it mean, Daddy?" Julia shouted toward the living room.

Fucking hell.

"It's just a bad way of showing you're mad at someone."

"Oh, okay," she answered, and thank everything, went back to watching her show.

"Thanks for that," I muttered to my idiot of a best friend.

Thatch just shrugged. "You know I can't be responsible for anything that comes out of my mouth right now."

"Your wife would have your ass if she knew suck it is now in your son's word repertoire two minutes into our minor-monitoring duty."

"Good thing he told your daughter because if Ace ever repeats it in front of Cassie, I'll just say he got it from your kid."

I shook my head and took a pull of my beer. "You have no shame."

"Especially when it comes to staying in my crazy wife's good graces," he added with a smirk.

I couldn't deny his logic. Cassie Kelly was…well, let's just say, I wouldn't want to be on the receiving end of her ire.

"Oh God," Thatch muttered and sat on the edge of the couch. "They're lining up. This is it. If Bailey doesn't pull through, I'll be at the Mavericks' offices on Monday morning protesting for a new owner."

"Just relax," I reassured, although, on the inside, I wasn't one hundred percent certain our quarterback could pull it off. Third down. Hardly any time left in the game. The pressure was on. And the Mavericks needed this win. It could be their make-it-or-break-it game to determine if they could pull off a Super Bowl run.

My words meant nothing. Thatch was on his feet and pacing the living room, every three steps his giant body blocking the entire screen.

"Could you sit down?" I asked, but it was too late, the ball had been snapped, and I found myself jumping around him to see the screen.

The offensive line held back Miami as Bailey searched for his open wide receiver.

He looked left. He looked right.

And then, just as one of Miami's best defensive ends broke through our line, Bailey locked on his target. Quick as a whip, he threw the ball down the field with precision and right into the hands of Sean Phillips—one of our best offensive weapons, who also happened to be Cassie's brother, therefore Thatch's brother-in-law.

"*Fuck yes!* Get it!" he shouted at the screen as Sean Phillips caught the ball, avoided a tackle with his famously quick feet, and eventually, found the open yards that led him straight into the end zone.

"*Touchdown!*" Thatch and I both cheered at the same time, high-fiving each other with giant grins on our faces.

Once we'd collected ourselves, I glanced back at the kids. Julia, Evie, and Ace appeared busy with drawing a picture together at the kitchen table—thankfully—and Gunner was still asleep in his swing.

"I think you dodged a bullet with the whole f-bomb shouting," I added with a nod toward the kids.

"What f-bomb shouting?" Thatch asked.

"You know, the part where you literally screamed it at the top of your lungs when Sean caught the ball?"

"I did?"

Jesus.

"Never mind."

"We've got Wes Lancaster here," the female sports reporter announced on the TV, and both Thatch's and my attention went right back to the screen. "It was a big night for the Mavericks tonight. Congratulations on the win."

"Thank you," he responded with a wide, very un-Wes-like grin.

I couldn't blame him; his team had pulled it out and were looking at a real chance of making it to the Super Bowl.

Life was good if you were Wes Lancaster right now.

"Is it safe to say tonight will be a night of celebration?"

Wes smirked and nodded. "I'm sure it will be for these guys, but I'm getting a little old for partying these days."

The reporter laughed and looked Wes over, clearly thinking he didn't look old at all.

"Wes better hope Winnie doesn't see that," Thatch muttered, and I chuckled.

"Well, the holiday is practically upon us. You must be doing at least a little celebrating for that," the reporter pushed.

Wes smiled but shook his head. "I'll be heading to a friend's cabin to celebrate Christmas with my wife and daughter and friends."

Quinn Bailey chimed in from behind him, his smiling, sweaty face now sharing the screen. "You don't want to spend Christmas with your boys, Lancaster?"

Wes chuckled. "There's nothing I want more, Quinn. I've been dreaming about it for years."

The reporter smiled and turned back to the screen while the celebration raged on behind her.

For some people, I guess Christmas came early.

CHAPTER 7

~~Rockin'~~ Boozin' Around the Christmas Tree

Georgia

With our husbands on kid duty, and my parents doing God knew what in their RV, Cassie and I had started to make some serious headway on the present-wrapping situation.

Honestly, I was shocked my best friend hadn't put up too much of a fight when I started getting one of the spare bedrooms all set up with scissors, ribbon, tape, and wrapping paper. Hell, she'd even helped me organize the gifts.

I had a feeling her willingness to go along with the schedule had more to do with the fact that my parents had decided to crash our holiday cabin party. I still didn't know who the culprits were who decided inviting Dick and Savannah was a good idea, but eventually, I'd find out. That was for damn sure. Even if I had to go CSI on this place, I'd figure it out. I wasn't above fucking fingerprints and polygraph tests.

"So, when was the last time you chatted with my mom?" I asked, and Cassie rolled her eyes as she folded red wrapping paper covered in snowflakes around a box that contained a toy truck for Ace.

"I swear on everything, I didn't tell your parents we were coming here."

"It's okay if you accidentally let it slip. I wouldn't be mad over something like that."

"First of all, that's a lie," she started with a perceptive smile. "And secondly, my lips have been sealed since we made these plans in November."

I sighed and wrapped a frilly gold bow around one of Evie's presents. "Then who told them? Was it Thatch?"

She laughed. "Thatch didn't even know we were coming to the Catskills until the night before we left."

"Are you serious? I told him the same day I told you!"

"He's a man, Wheorgie. He'd lose his cock if it weren't attached to his body."

I cringed. "That's an awful visual you're giving."

"But it's the fluffing truth," she reiterated. "And that says a lot considering a man's most prized possession is his dick."

"I don't think Kline would lose his dick if it weren't attached."

"That's because your husband is some kind of fucking hybrid," she retorted with a snort. "Believe me, a man who is calm, cool, collected, and completely patient with your hyper, neurotic ass while you're working through a notebook full of holiday itineraries and to-do lists is a one-in-a-million kind of man."

"I'm not hyper or neurotic."

She flashed a knowing smirk in my direction.

"Okay, fine," I relented. "Maybe I'm a little of both. But it comes from a good place. I just want everyone to have an amazing Christmas."

"Just a little?"

"Shut up." I tossed the tape at her head, and she ducked out of the way on a laugh.

After she finished wrapping Ace's toy truck, she grabbed her mug of eggnog from the table and took a hearty, lip-smacking sip. "I know Dick and Savannah weren't supposed to be here, but your mom makes killer eggnog."

I groaned, but considering I was on glass number three, I couldn't deny my mom's eggnog had always been one of my favorite parts of the holidays growing up. Most Christmases, Will and I would beg them to let us have more than the one allotted glass.

"Between the nog and the delicious fudge and holiday candies she made this afternoon, I'm starting to wonder if she's trying to make me feel guilty for attempting to have a quiet, relaxed Christmas without them," I said on a sigh and looked at Cass. I could feel the tinglings of regret slowly seeping into my soul. "Am I horrible person for attempting to have two separate Christmases?"

"Fluff no." She snorted and shook her head, her long, brown hair shaking softly across her shoulders. "Dick's holiday display of crazy set the roof on fire, and he ended up in the ER last year. Pretty sure your original plan of enjoying Christmas Day without needing the assistance of emergency personnel was warranted."

God, I loved her.

"I love you," I said between sips of eggnog. Because I did. I loved her.

She paused mid-wrap and blew me a kiss. "I love you too."

"Like, I really love you."

"Samesies," she agreed as her fingers struggled to get the tape out of the dispenser. "If I ever divorce Thatch or we move to a place where polygamy is legal, I hope you'll be my wife."

"Pfffft, like you'd ever divorce Thatch. God, I couldn't imagine my life without Kline. He's my favorite ever."

Cassie gave up on the tape and twirled her hair. "I lover T."

"I lover Kline. And you. Oh, and my kids. Fuck, I almost

forgot about them."

She nodded and continued the hair-twirling. "Your kids are great."

"I know. I love Julia and..." I paused and searched for the other name. Fuck, what was her name? "And...and...Ev...Eva... Evie! Yes, I love my little Evie!"

Shit. Is that bad mom material?

"They're beautiful girls. Just like you." Cassie winked and pointed a slow and slightly sloppy index finger in my direction. I figured her fingers were probably just tired from fighting the tape.

"*You're* beautiful."

Cassie smiled. "I know.

"I like your kids too." Because I did. I really liked her kids.

Cass stared at me. And stared at me. And then... "Oh yeah, *my* kids. Ace and Gunner. They're great. I mean, they can be assholes, but I love 'em. And it's really only two-fourths their fault. Assholes coming from assholes' trees and all that shit." She twirled her hair again, and I had the urge to feel it. My best friend had gorgeous hair.

"Your hair is pretty. Can I touch it?"

She nodded. "Uh-huh."

I reached out and ran my fingers through the silky ends. "It's soft too. You should be a hair model."

"You should too."

Man, my best friend is my best friend.

I giggled.

This room is funny.

"Can I hug you?"

"Yep," Cass said and held out both arms, and we hugged. The wrapping paper crinkled beneath our feet, but I was sure it would be fine.

Hugging is so fun.

"Knock knock." My mother peeked her head in with two glasses and a silver tray in her hands. "I thought I'd stop in, say hello, and see if you ladies would like some more eggnog?" she asked, and I silently prayed she didn't start oversharing the details of her afternoon spent with my father in their RV.

Lucky for me, my best friend's enthusiasm forced my mother's attention elsewhere.

"That'd be fluffing fantastic!" Cassie exclaimed as she picked up an empty roll of wrapping paper and pointed it toward my mother. She fired off a few fake shots in the direction of the door and exclaimed, "Pow-pow, motherfluffers!"

I laughed. And she laughed. And then, just like magic, we had more eggnog.

Cassie took a healthy gulp from her glass and let out a little *ah* sound from her lips. "This is good shit." She gave my mother a thumbs-up. "I want this recipe."

"Sure thing, sweetheart." Savannah smiled and wrapped her arms around both of us. "The secret is in the perfect mix of nutmeg, cognac, and bourbon."

I giggled again. *Nutmeg. Nuts. I should probably lick Kline's—Wait...what? Did she just say cognac and bourbon?*

My eyes went wide, and Cassie just started cracking up. Hell, she was cackling.

No wonder I'd forgotten my kid's name. I was drunk! We were both drunk!

Jesus, that explains the hugging and hair-petting...

"Are you kidding me?" I shouted.

"What?" my mother questioned in confusion. "I thought you loved my eggnog. You and Will used to fight over it when you were kids."

"Oh my God, Mom! Tell me you were giving us a different, less boozy version back in the day!"

"The alcohol makes the nog, Georgie," she explained without an inkling of concern or guilt, or you know, a normal motherly emotion related to giving her children booze.

"We were kids!" I shouted and took a quick glance into my glass, and then immediately set it back down, far, *far* away from me. I honestly had no idea how she did it, but I knew I didn't need any more of it. That fluffing nog didn't reveal even a hint of booze. It was like my mother knew some kind of witchcraft-alcohol-camouflage secret that no one else knew.

With the way she snuck liquor into her holiday drinks, if she handed me a brownie, you could bet your sweet ass I was declining.

"It was one glass, sweetheart." She let out an exasperated sigh. "Don't be so dramatic. And you were both kids that got rambunctious on Christmas. The eggnog served as a little sedative to calm you two down."

"Oh my God! It's a wonder I survived my childhood without needing rehab."

Cassie continued to alternate between giggles and cackles. I wanted to smack her. And hug her.

Goddamn eggnog.

My entire childhood flashed before my eyes. So much for heartfelt holiday memories. While other kids were playing with their new toys, I had been unknowingly begging my parents for more booze.

"No wonder these presents look like I had Ace wrap them. I thought it was the fact that I'd been doing the activity against my will, but this makes even more sense. Your mom got us drunk, Wheorgie," Cassie announced, grinned, and then without another thought, took another hearty drink.

"Stop drinking it!"

"It's too late now. I'm already going to have to pump and

dump." Cass shrugged and raised her glass to my mom. "Cheers, Savannah."

"Cheers, sweetheart," my mother returned the sentiment kindly. "And what do you mean, pump and dump? I used to breast-feed Will and Georgia all the time after a few glasses of wine."

"Of course you breastfed us after you went on a wine bender!" I exclaimed in outrage. "Hell, did you put cocaine in our Cheerios to wake us up in the morning too?"

My mother tsked under her breath. "Oh, don't be so ridiculous, Georgia."

Ridiculous? She breastfed us after drinking wine and gave my brother and me actual booze when we were kids. *Oh yeah, I'm definitely the ridiculous one in this scenario.*

"Considering I'm on like glass number six of this eggnog," Cassie started to explain, "pretty sure I'd be better off feeding Gunner from a tapped keg at this point, Savannah."

While I sat there, surrounded by torn-up wrapping paper, half-assed bows, and a pathetic looking display of gifts that were supposed to be ready to put under the tree, my best friend drank it up with my mother.

They laughed and gabbed, and I lay back in the pile of shredded wrapping scraps and played with my hair. I wanted to rage, but I didn't have it in me. There was too much cognac and bourbon in my veins.

The two of them ignored me.

Eventually, after Cassie had downed glass number *too fucking many*, she shouted toward the door, "Thatcher! Kline! Get your asses up here!"

I wasn't sure of the exact elapsed time, but I was pretty sure they came running. Thatch peeked his head through the door. "What's up, Crazy?"

"Are the kids in bed?"

Not for long if you yell across the house like a psychopath again,
I mused.

"Yep," he responded, and Kline appeared behind him.

"Fan-fluffing-tastic," she responded. "Because we're too drunk
to wrap."

Thatch's brow rose. "What?"

"I said, *we're too drunk to wrap.*"

"I heard that. I'm just trying to figure out how." He glanced
around the room while Kline walked over toward me and picked
up my glass. He sniffed it and then looked at me in my pile of piti-
ful in confusion.

"My childhood is a sham," I muttered.

He quirked a brow, and Cassie burst into laughter again. Kline
offered a hand, a sweet smirk on his face and pulled me to sitting.
Cassie's laughter renewed as I pulled a piece of scrap paper from
my bedraggled hair.

"Stop laughing!"

She snorted, and I shoved her shoulder until she fell into the
neat grouping of wrapping paper rolls behind her. They bounced
and tumbled everywhere.

"Benny?" Kline asked, and I groaned, my shoulders sagging.

"My mom has been giving me booze since I was a kid, and I
think I need therapy."

He looked at my mom, and she shrugged her shoulders. "She's
mad because I let her and Willy have a glass of eggnog a couple of
times when they were kids."

"A couple of times? It was every Christmas!"

"It was just one glass, sweetheart," she reassured.

I looked at my husband. "I think I'm an alcoholic. I need
Triple A."

"I think you mean AA, honey," Thatch interjected as he helped
Cassie out of the wreckage.

"Shut up," I mumbled. "I can't help it that my mom got me hammered on the down low."

Kline bit his bottom lip, and this time, held out both hands to help me to my feet.

The bastard was one second away from laughing. At me. His wife.

"Don't laugh," I demanded.

He wiped his face clean and rubbed my upper arms. "I'm not laughing, baby."

I glared, and he averted his eyes.

Fluffing turncoat.

"I'm laughing," Cass cackled. "Fuck, I love your family, Georgie."

That was it. I was going to smack her. I started to move toward her and let the threats fly past my lips, but Thatcher, the stupid protective husband, pulled her behind his ginormous back. "I'm going to kick your ask…as…asssssss."

Fuck, I'm drunk.

Kline wrapped his arms around my shoulders before I could make good on my promise, while Thatch lifted his wife up and threw her over his shoulders with a giant grin on his face. "C'mon, Crazy. It's time for bed."

"Night, guys!" Cassie gave me a thumbs-up as her husband carried her out of the guest room, and I looked around the room at the awful display of wrapped presents. I could actually see by the stacks of gifts at what point in the evening we'd started to get drunk.

"What am I going to do?" I looked at Kline. "These gifts look like shit, and I'm drunk."

"Don't worry, sweetheart," my mother interjected as she started to unstack one of the shitty piles. "I'll work on these before I go to bed."

Oh, now she wanted to help me. Where was this kind of mind-set before she decided to get me drunk?

"I've got an idea," Kline responded and lifted me into his arms. "How about you get into bed, and I'll come back downstairs and fix the gifts with your mom?"

"You'd do that?" I said on a half whine, half slur. "But it's probably so much work."

He shrugged and carried me toward our bedroom. "Don't you already know, Benny girl?"

"Know what?" I asked, and he smiled down at me as he walked me toward our bed.

"I'd do anything to make you happy."

I smiled.

Good Lord, this man is really mine?

I knew I should've said more words. But the eggnog. And goodness gracious, the bed felt so good as he tucked me into it. I made a mental note to say all the things tomorrow, but right now, I had to sleep off the booze.

CHAPTER 8

A ~~Holly Jolly~~ "Holy Shit, Georgie's Going to Lose It" Christmas

Kline

December 24th, Christmas Eve Morning

Georgia's skin hummed with warmth as I touched my lips to the apple of her cheek and, trying not to disturb her, slowly shoved myself out of bed.

She was still out—fucking cold—but last night had been a big one for her. And, all things considered, I thought she was handling the changes to her guest list pretty well.

The halls were quiet, thanks to equally exhausted kids and adults looking to take advantage of that glorious situation, as I made my way down to the kitchen and fired up the sixteen-cup coffeepot. It might have seemed like overkill, brewing the max amount, but my Georgie could drink half the fucking thing on her own—and today, she would need to.

Grabbing the paper from the front drive as quietly as

possible—the door was new but still had a squeak—and settling in at the kitchen table, I opened up to the sports section and read what the sports critics had to say about the Mavericks game.

It wasn't all flattering—it never was—but with another win in the books, the boys had made it hard for the nitpickers to find too much to complain about.

I peeked around the paper as the coffee stopped gurgling. Full pot. Fantastic.

Folding the paper back to rights, I tossed it in a stack on the table and grabbed a mug from the cabinet to pour Georgia a cup, when the squeaky door alerted me to a new arrival.

"Hello?" Wes called into the house on a shouted whisper. "Anyone awake?"

I set the mug on the counter and scooted around the wall and down the hall quickly to try to prevent yelling. He'd been considerate on the first attempt, but I knew my friends, and there was nothing in our history to show he'd be the same on a second.

"Hey, Wes," I called when he came into view, and his eyes, previously scanning the upstairs landing, jumped to me.

"Hey, man. I was beginning to think everybody was still asleep."

"I'm not. They are," I said with a smirk. "Seems Dick and Savannah made it up here, after all."

"Oh my God," Winnie breathed as she stepped around Wes. "Georgia must be freaking."

I leaned forward to give her a kiss on the cheek and then put my fist out for a bump from their ten-year-old daughter, Lexi. She obliged.

"Yeah," I said with a groan. "She's not thrilled, but she's dealing."

I turned back to Wes. "You wouldn't know anything about how they happened to find out we were coming here, would you?"

"What? How would I know anything about Dick and Savannah?"

I shrugged and slid my hands into the pockets of my pants. "Someone had to have told them."

"Well, it wasn't me."

"He's not lying," Lex interjected. "He did tell the entirety of the Mavericks, though."

Wes's eyes closed, and his head dropped back as I cut hard eyes to him.

"What?"

"Relax. Bailey got talkative after the win and asked where we were going. I told him the Catskills, but nothing more than that."

My shoulders sank slightly, moving a notch closer to normal. They'd need more information than that to find us and a hell of a lot of motivation. We were safe.

I jerked my head toward the kitchen and escorted their family of three farther into the house. "At least I can count on Lex to keep me in the loop."

Winnie laughed, and Wes tucked Lex close to his front. "I know. The kid is all honesty. I keep trying to break the habit, but she just won't give."

Lex rolled her eyes. "Dad."

"Sorry, sorry," Wes apologized with a chuckle.

I caught sight of the abandoned mug on the counter and jumped back into action. "You guys make yourselves at home, get some coffee." I grabbed the pot and held it up before pouring a piping hot stream into Georgie's mug. "I'm gonna run this up to my hungover wife, and then I'll be back down."

"Hungover?" Winnie questioned with a pout. "They got drunk without me?"

Lex rolled her eyes again, and I chuckled. "Not by choice."

Wes's eyebrows drew together, and he scoffed. "Well, that sure sounds like a story."

"It is. I'll tell you all about it when I come back down."

They nodded in acknowledgment, and I headed for the stairs. I listened hard at the top for any sounds from either one of my daughters, but everything was still quiet, so I moved on down the hall and into the bedroom at the end.

Georgia had shifted to her stomach, one long leg cocked high and out of the covers. I set the cup of coffee on the nightstand and sat down in the bed next to her.

I stroked her skin from shin to thigh until her eyes peeked open. As soon as we made visual contact, I leaned down and touched my lips to hers.

She squeaked, jumped back, and covered her mouth. "I haven't brushed my teeth yet," she mumbled behind her hand.

I shook my head, but she went on.

"My mouth tastes like rotten sewage."

"Wow." I chuckled. "Lovely visual, baby."

"So, trust me, you want me to brush my teeth."

She was forgetting the fact that she was *my* wife. Nothing could prevent me from kissing her. *Even* morning breath.

I pretended to think about it briefly before pulling her hand away and kissing her again. She fought it for about a second before forgetting herself and kissing me back in a way only my wife could. It was earth-shifting—life-altering. Every single time.

"I love you," she whispered just as I thought it myself, her lips against mine.

I nodded and put my lips to her ear. She shivered. "Baby, you have no idea."

She hummed and snuggled close, and I fought against the urge to climb into bed with her and show her how much.

"Wes, Winnie, and Lex are here," I said into the curve of her neck.

She nearly jumped out of her skin. "Oh my God, they are? What time is it?"

The duvet jerked back and forth as she moved frantically, unable to decide which side of the bed would be faster to climb out of.

"Relax, baby, it's fine."

She glared. "Time, Kline."

"It's nine."

"Nine?" she shrieked. "I was supposed to be up two hours ago! I have to make the pancake batter and move that fucking elf. Julia will have a shit hemorrhage if that fucking thing doesn't move!"

That fucking elf, otherwise known as Antonio, *our* Elf on the Shelf. The idea of that thing made me grin and cringe at the same time. It was one of those new-age holiday traditions that was oddly adorable for kids, but when you had to deal with the actual logistics of remembering to secretly move the damn thing to a new location, *every fucking morning*, it quickly became a pain in the ass.

"Georgie," I soothed, grabbing her chin and turning it toward me softly. "Relax. I brought you coffee." I nodded to the mug, and she glanced at it longingly as the picture of having coffee in bed played out in her mind. "Take your time, get dressed, get some coffee in you, and then come downstairs. I'll make sure Antonio the elf is moved and get the girls when they wake up, okay? I can't say that I'll start the pancake batter, but, baby, the way you make pancakes, I guarantee the crowd will wait."

Her voice was wistful as her eyes searched mine. "Why do you love me?"

I shook my head. "Too many reasons to list now, love. It's already nine," I teased.

She rolled her eyes but sighed sweetly. "I'm so, so lucky. You're so loving and generous and put up with my excitement."

Excitement. What a cute name for hysteria.

I nodded. "And I've got a big dick. Don't forget that one."

"Kline!"

"Baby, it's in my name."

"Big-dick Brooks is *not* your actual name!"

"People address me as such."

She scoffed. "Cassie doesn't count."

"It counts." I scooped her up and pulled her to my lap, fingers digging into her perfect ass. It was nearly bare thanks to her lacy, cheeky underwear, and I almost groaned. "And later, I'm gonna show you how good I am at using it too."

When I got back downstairs, I went about moving the elf and setting up a snowball fight with marshmallows for the kids with Lex's help. I hadn't intended to spoil the whole elf illusion for her, but she'd laughed when I hinted to Winnie to maybe occupy her somewhere else. Apparently, thinking the Elf on the Shelf was a real thing was for people at least three years younger than her—and of a much lesser intelligence.

Georgie came down half an hour later, and I had to hide my smile behind my coffee mug *and* the paper. She looked beautiful, as always, but it was more than apparent that she'd hurried.

Wes averted his eyes, smart enough to know a comment from her boss would not be welcome, as Winnie jumped up and pulled Georgie's skirt from its spot—tucked into her underwear.

"Oh my God," Georgia shouted, and Winnie shushed her. "Relax, it's fine. No one saw."

Wes and I had both seen, but the kitchen table had never looked more interesting to either of us.

"Good morning!" Thatch boomed as he stepped into the

kitchen, a pair of red pants, a white dress shirt, and a red satin bow tie completing his ensemble.

"Good God," Wes mumbled.

Thatch smiled a toothy grin and leaned down to whisper in Wes's ear. "Don't be so jealous, Whitney. I'm an anomaly. No one else can look this good. It's isn't just you."

"Does everyone want pancakes?" Georgia asked, her blush of embarrassment just then starting to come under control. At least Thatch hadn't been in the room for the tucked skirt incident. I had a feeling he would have been markedly more vocal than Wes and me.

"I already had some breakfast," Thatch said suggestively, waggling his eyebrows. Wes dry heaved. "But I could eat some more."

"Yeah, Daddy," Cassie said as she entered the room while she was still pulling down her shirt. I looked back to the table to avoid seeing nipple.

"Let's all cool it with the *exsay* talk, okay?" Georgia ordered. "The kids will be up soon."

Translation for all of you who don't speak Pig Latin.
Exsay = Sexy.
Not something I thought I'd ever become fluent in, but that's life with kids.

Cassie and Thatch both looked around casually.

"Huh. Look at that, Thatcher. Our kids aren't here."

"Jesus Christ, how are they parents?" Wes asked the room as if they weren't there.

They weren't offended as one might think. Instead, Cassie shrugged. "Beats the hell out of me."

"I think it's because I uckfayed you without an ondomcay," Thatch pointed out helpfully, and Georgie glared over her shoulder.

I chuckled, and the glare shifted to me.

"Sorry, baby, but that was funny," I admitted.

Sudden and harsh, two beeps of an industrial-sized horn filled the air and made every single one of us jump.

"Holy fluff. What the fluff was that?" Thatch asked.

I shrugged. Wes and Winnie exchanged a panicked look. My eyebrows drew together.

"Do you know—" I started to ask Wes, but he shook his head desperately.

Pounding shook the front door and startled us again, and anxiety in her eyes, Georgia took off like a shot toward the front entry. It took the rest of us a half-second longer, but we all followed. Thatch and Cassie tried to go through the doorway to the hall at the same time and got into a minor argument about who was going to go first, trapping us all in the kitchen until I shoved them out of the way.

My wife was out there alone facing God knew what. Horrible visions of Dick driving that giant RV toward my wife and the side of the mountain danced in my head.

I ran down the hall and got to the jam-packed foyer just as a sleepy Julia put her hands to the spindles upstairs and let out a shriek when her eyes peered out the giant floor-to-ceiling window looking over the front of the house. "Oh my goshs. Mavericks!" She turned her head back to the hall and yelled, "Evie! Gunner! Ace! The Mavericks is heres!"

Holy fucking shit.

One by one and with duffel bags in hand, they walked off a huge tour-style bus and toward our front door.

Quinn Bailey's smile was magnetic as he did a rolling bow, worthy of the royals, in front of my shell-shocked wife. The rest of the team—or by my exact count, seven other players—chuckled.

Sean Phillips waved toward his sister Cassie and Thatch.

Cam Mitchell grinned at the kids who were now awake and hopping around on the porch, shouting their excitement.

And my wife, well, she was gone.

Literally gone. Georgia passed out cold. Boom. Just like that, she made like a dead fish and flopped toward the floor.

I wasn't in range to catch her, but thankfully, she had nearly a whole football team who was.

Merry fucking Christmas.

CHAPTER 9

~~Santa Claus~~ Santa's Dick Is Coming to Town

Georgia

What was supposed to be a quiet little Christmas Eve with my husband, daughters, and closest friends had turned into a cabin filled with what felt like half of the Mavericks football team and my dad prancing around the house in his favorite pair of thermal underwear. *Keep your friends close and your dicks closer,* I could hear him saying now while Quinn Bailey, Cassie's brother Sean, Cam Mitchell, and a handful of other huge, tree trunk-thighed men laughed. Apparently, our cabin in the Catskills had become Dick's stage, and he was tossing out dad jokes like he was trying to win a gig on Comedy Central.

Where had everything gone wrong? First, Dick and Savannah showing up apropos of nothing, and now, the football team. I mean, it wasn't the entire Mavericks football team, but still, it was too much chaos, too many people, and I had my doubts that this many uninvited guests could have found their way here without help.

Sabotage.

Skeptical, I glanced around the room, taking in all of the possible suspects.

Cassie, Thatch, Wes, Winnie, my freakin' husband, the list of prospective defectors had my head spinning.

My gut instinct and my heart told me my husband wasn't in on the scam. He was a man who lived his life with two priorities: keeping his family happy and safe. Obviously, ruining my Christmas plans would not equal a happy wife. Nor would it equate to *his* safety.

Would my best girlfriends really try to fuck up Christmas?

Win might've been a bit of a hard-ass in the locker room, but she was a softy to her core. I couldn't rule out the possibility that it was her, though. She was a mom, had been one longer than the rest of us, and sometimes mothers do things based on what they *think* is best. I'd have to keep my eye on her.

Cassie was notorious for pranks, but she knew how important this holiday was to me, not to mention, she'd seen me at my craziest moments. She might've been spontaneous and impulsive, but she did have *some* self-preservation. Right?

"Come on, Thatcher, smack it harder," she yelled from the back porch. I glanced outside to see that they'd set up a piñata for the kids—but were partaking themselves.

Maybe she doesn't have any sense of self-preservation.

The odds of Thatcher inviting my parents and the entire goddamn football team were slim to none, considering he knew his wife would murder him in his sleep if he pulled off this horrible of a prank on her nearest and dearest friend without her help—which of course, didn't rule them out as a team.

Wes wasn't normally the type of guy to meddle in someone else's plans, but he was ruthless in business and controlled any and every aspect of his football team, so I supposed he had it in him.

Basically, I had too many leads without enough strategy, and everyone was still a possible suspect.

Aside from Kline. Because, honestly, if he was involved, I hoped I never found out. I needed him too much to divorce him, and a marriage without sex—because I'd have to punish him somehow—sounded like pure torture.

"Stop looking at everyone like you're thirty seconds away from bringing out a polygraph test," Cassie muttered under her breath as she gently nudged me with her elbow, obviously having come inside from the back porch. I glanced out the window to see Thatch assisting Julia as she swung a broomstick wildly.

Was it possible to order a polygraph test on Christmas Eve? Surely, Amazon still had free shipping with Prime...

"Seriously. Georgia. Take a breath."

I looked away from the living room that held eight too many fucking football players and met Cassie's eyes. "I'm fine."

"You're the exact opposite of fine."

I rolled my eyes. "I'm fine."

"You're completely pissed off right now," she whispered.

I shrugged. "I'm just disappointed." I glanced at the giant, rustic clock hanging above the mantle. It was half past four. Now, prior to everything falling apart, we would be finishing up ice skating and drinking hot chocolate. But since the players couldn't risk injury, and Lex and my father wouldn't leave their side—and Wes wouldn't leave Lex's side, and Winnie wouldn't leave his, and *so on*—the original perfectly planned-out Christmas agenda had flown out the window faster than my dad was tossing out jokes.

Cassie wrapped her arm around my shoulder. "It's all going to be okay, honey."

"That's what you said when my parents parked a house on wheels in my front yard, and look what happened after that.

Practically an entire professional football team showed up unannounced."

"Well…if it makes you feel any better…unless your dad starts telling jokes naked, I highly doubt it could get any worse at this point."

I groaned. "Are you trying to jinx me?"

She laughed quietly, and I glared.

"Okay. Okay. I take back the words I just said—"

"It's too late for that. They've already been unleashed into the universe. Surely, they are already working their black magic to ruin what's left of this Christmas."

She ignored my words. "I want you to realize one thing," she said and held me closer to her side, "you have a cabin filled with everyone you love the most, and you know what?"

"What?" I asked, petulance seeping from my voice.

"Every single one of these people loves you too. Crazy. Insane. Adoring kind of love. You're the reason we're all here together to celebrate Christmas."

I was pretty sure I was not the reason for the football players, but I was becoming more and more suspicious of Cassie. She kept trying to make all this shit *all right*.

She's supposed to be commiserating with me!

"It's the truth, Georgia," she reaffirmed her words. "Just remember that."

"Ugh. You're making too much sense right now," I said and let out a long and exasperated breath as I wiggled out of her hold and headed for the kitchen. "Go drink some eggnog or something."

"Man, oh man, I forgot how sassy pissed-off Wheorgie is." Cassie grinned.

I flipped her the middle finger as I opened the fridge to figure out how in the hell I was going to feed all of these people. Sure, the pancake situation at breakfast was easy to solve, but dinner? Not so much. It was the complete opposite. I'd planned out a delicious, gourmet meal for six adults and five kids, but I hadn't calculated enough food for that number to very nearly double.

It was almost five p.m., and panic was starting to really set in.

What were all of these people going to eat?

Cripes, where in the hell were they going to sleep tonight?

I just needed a minute. Hell, maybe I needed an hour.

A few quiet and relaxing moments, far away from punch lines and my dad's thermal underwear, were exactly what the doctor would probably order for me right now.

The doctor being someone who was a psychiatrist who was trying to avoid committing me to a psych ward.

With a quick glance back into the living room, I noted that my mother had Evie in her lap and Kline had Julia on his shoulders. Yeah, I could definitely steal a few moments away for myself before I spontaneously combusted from anxiety.

The instant I reached our bedroom, I shut the door and threw myself onto the bed with a groan.

For the next few minutes, I alternated between praying, screaming into a pillow, and crying.

I felt so damn emotional, if it weren't for the fact that I was on birth control and I'd just finished my period a few days ago, I'd be wondering if I was pregnant.

Somehow, someway, I had to find a way to slap a smile on my face and work through the roadblocks that were now affecting my Christmas Eve agenda.

Things like: How could I feed an extra ten mouths? Where could I find enough pillows, blankets, and air mattresses to sleep half a football team? Or, what was the safest way to lock my father in a closest to proactively prevent a fire or explosion or something else equally as terrible?

I ran through the list of issues in search of solutions, and by the time I'd repeated the same thought process with the same, no-answer results, I decided that maybe I just needed some na-maste in my life.

I was thirty seconds into Downward-Facing Dog when a con-versation I never thought I'd hear reached my fucking ears.

"Ace! Ace! Come see Santa's Dick!" My daughter's voice echoed off the walls and straight into my bedroom.

"Santa's Dick?" Ace questioned. "Where, Lia?"

"Downstairs! Come downstairs and see Santa's Dick!"

Santa's Dick?

What in the ever-loving fuck was happening?

Little footsteps ran past my bedroom and down the wooden staircase, and I went from downward dog to upward mom on the warpath in mere seconds.

"Kline!" I shouted as I jogged down the stairs. "Kline!"

Please, for the love of God, tell me my husband has control over whatever the hell is happening right now!

At the bottom of the stairs, I came skidding to a stop as a blur of red streaked by me and into the living room. Dick Cummings, my father and former stand-up comedian, dressed up as Santa Claus.

Santa. Dick.

Oh. My. God.

First of all, I really needed to work a little harder with Julia and the whole extra S with every damn word situation. And sec-ondly, I needed to force my heart back into a normal rhythm.

I held a hand to my chest and took a few deep breaths. When that didn't work, I took twenty more and closed my eyes. By the time I'd calmed down enough not to feel like I was going to go into some sort of cardiac arrest, Santa Dick was already passing out what appeared to be sheet music to everyone in the group, while the kids danced around him chanting, "Say Ho Ho Ho!"

Of course, Santa Dick obliged. "Ho! Ho! Ho! Merry Christmas!"

"Yay!" Julia squealed. "Is it time for songs now?"

"It sure is, little lady," my dad responded, and I wasn't sure if I wanted to scream or cry.

Lucky for me, it was at that exact moment that my husband came up behind me and wrapped his arms around my shoulders. "You doing okay, baby?" he whispered into my ear, and I shook my head.

He turned me in his arms and pressed me close to his chest while everyone inside the house started the first, very off-key lyrics of "We Wish You a Merry Christmas."

Air filled my lungs again, and the burn in my chest evaporated.

Sometimes, when things weren't going as planned, you really just needed a hug from your person. And Kline, he was definitely *my* person.

"Can I tell you a secret?" he whispered into my ear, and I leaned back to meet his eyes.

"You bought us another cabin farther up the mountain that we can go stay in right now?"

He smirked and shook his head. "I called in some favors. Ones that might earn me some of a sexual nature a little later."

"What kind of favors?" I questioned, even as an excited shiver ran through me. "Tell me you didn't order Santa's Dick a prostitute?"

"Fucking hell," he choked through a laugh. "We really need to get her to cool it with the extra S's."

"You're telling me," I responded. "When I heard her tell Ace to come downstairs to see Santa's Dick, I nearly croaked."

Kline chuckled. "I thought Thatch had made another gargoyle dick faux pas."

I rolled my eyes, but my body tingled as happy memories

assaulted me. Secrets and firsts and everything else that led me to this moment, in this man's arms.

"So," I said and nudged my hip against his, "what about these favors?"

"The rest of the meals over the next two days will be catered, by a renowned chef out of the city *not* with the Meals on Wheels establishment, and I managed to fix the sleeping situation."

A laugh bubbled out of me. "Thank you." I didn't even know what to say. Normally, I would've asked him one million questions about how he managed it and inquired about the exact details of everything, but I was just too damn relieved that my husband knew I was about to break, and he took it upon himself to find a solution. "Just…thank you."

He touched his mouth to mine.

God, I'm so fucking lucky.

Tears pricked my eyes. I couldn't help it. Always doting, devoted, and thoughtful to his core, my husband was my fucking person. *Always.*

"Don't cry," he whispered and pressed a soft kiss to one cheek and then the other.

"These aren't sad tears."

"I love you, Georgia girl."

"I love you too," I whispered back. "So much."

"All right, baby…" Kline smiled and held out his hand as he moved back toward the living room. "I think it's time we join in on the Christmas carol fun."

By the time we reached the group, they had moved on to "Jingle Bells."

"Georgie! Kline!" Santa Dick shouted toward us. "You're late to the caroling party! Grab some sheet music, and get with the holiday program!"

Cool it, Santa Dick.

Dressed head to toe in red velvet with a big white beard rest-ing at the very top of his rotund belly while leading—*more like forcing*—our big group into another Christmas carol, my father was out of fluffing control.

But a girl could only handle so many panic attacks in a twen-ty-four span of time, so the only thing I could do was sing along with Santa Dick.

"Jingle bells! Jingle bells! Jingle all the way…" he sang at the top of his lungs. "C'mon, Cassie!" Dick nodded reassuringly in my best friend's direction and patted his big, fluffy stomach. "Santa can't hear that beautiful voice of yours! Jingle *all* the way, sweet-heart! Nobody likes a half-assed jingler. Ain't that right, Georgie?"

All I could do was sigh internally, but Cassie's reaction was far more volatile. She glared right into Santa's jolly eyes. "Suck it, Santa Dick."

It was safe to say I wasn't the only one ready to strangle Santa with my bare hands.

"Suck it!" Ace repeated his mother's words.

"Ah, man, Cass," Thatch chimed in. "Watch the language around the kids, honey."

She glared directly at her husband, and before additional, very colorful, completely inappropriate words could fly from my best friend's lips, I did the only thing I could do in that moment. I started singing. At the top of my lungs.

"Jingle bells! Jingle bells! Jingle all the way!"

Thank everything that it only took half of the first verse be-fore everyone else was singing along with me.

Sometimes you just had to give in to the insanity and make the best of it, right?

CHAPTER 10

<del>White</del> Chaotic Christmas

Kline

December 25th, Christmas Morning

Morning light bled into the windows and danced as trees in the yard cut in front of the sun and back again. I reached out and patted across the space on the bed beside me.

Empty.

Where was my wife?

I'd expected her to be here after the workout we'd put in last night, after how hard she'd come—*all three times.*

I looked up at the headboard and smiled at the small tear in the upholstery she'd put there.

Back arched and moans getting louder, Georgia ground down on my face as she neared her second orgasm. My face was soaked, and I had a brief thought that I would keep it that way, unwashed, so all it would take was a lick whenever I wanted a taste of her.

I groaned as a new rush of wetness flooded my mouth and

*swallowed it down, my dick aching to be inside her so bad he'd start-
ed to make signs for a formal protest.*

*I flicked my tongue against her clit and then swirled, stopping
at the bottom to push it inside her.*

*Her pussy spasmed and she shook, her hands clutching violently
into the fabric of the headboard.*

*"Oh my God!" she exclaimed on an angry whisper. "My nail
went through!"*

*I smiled against her pussy, still firmly resting on my face, but
that didn't stop her from seeing the amusement in my eyes.*

*"Kline!" she snapped. "This is a thousand-dollar headboard,
and I just put a hole in it."*

*I lifted her up and flipped her to her back so suddenly, she
gasped.*

*"I'm not worried about the hole in the headboard. I'm worried
about the hole in* you *and how I'm gonna fill it."*

I smiled again as I remembered her scandalized face, and my
dick jerked at the memory of the soft heat that had followed. She'd
needed the release, and God, I'd needed to give it to her. But apparently, even that much pleasure hadn't completely unwound her.

I hopped from the bed and pulled on a pair of pajama pants,
not bothering with underwear or a shirt, and went in search of my
Georgie.

The house was quiet, much like the morning before, but I
knew it wouldn't be long before some hyped kids came somer-
saulting down the stairs, demanding to be shown to their presents.

At the bottom of the staircase, the bodies started—not dead,
thankfully—and I danced and weaved accordingly. Only the last,
Mr. Quarterback himself, Quinn Bailey, presented a challenge, as
he slumbered laterally in front of the doorway to the kitchen. I
considered my options only briefly before stepping directly over
his giant frame.

Still out like a light, most likely worn-out from one too many jokes from my father-in-law, he didn't notice.

I was glad they were there, even if they made the house feel much smaller than it was. Wes had explained shortly after their arrival that the players who'd shown up all lived outside of the New York area and didn't really have time to go home for the holidays. Their next game was a week out, but evening practices started back up the day after Christmas. They could have rushed a flight home and back again, but nobody really wanted to spend their Christmas Eve and Day in the airport for a completely unfulfilling visit. Coming to the cabin had been a win-win situation for everyone—Sean got to spend time with his sister, and the rest of them got to spend time with people who cared about them.

"Good morning, baby," I greeted and took my time perusing the gorgeous creature in front of me. Her long, blond hair hung loosely down her back, ending a scant inch above the silky fabric of her pajama camisole. I smiled when I reached the luscious curves of her ass covered by a pair of her favorite Christmas-themed sleep leggings.

Have mercy.

She turned at the sound of my voice, a coffee mug in her hand, and raised one pointed eyebrow. "When you said you had the sleeping situation figured out, I didn't think you meant every available inch of surface area on our floor."

I shrugged with a cheeky grin. "It's working, isn't it?"

She inclined her head in agreement. "Look, Kline. I know I've been a little—"

"Crazy?" I offered.

She turned back toward the coffeemaker, but I didn't miss the scowl that covered her full lips.

"*Overanxious,*" she corrected, and I couldn't help but smile at how adorable she was.

"Right," I agreed, leaning a hip into the counter and crossing my arms over my chest and my feet at the ankles.

"I just wanted everything to be perfect," she admitted.

Practically at that exact moment, the screeching started.

"It's Christ-masssss! Presents! Santa-s Dick! La la la la la la!"

"Lia! Lia! Do you see any presents with my name?"

I didn't take my eyes off of Georgie's face as hers closed slowly in acceptance of her *overanxious* moments that had occurred during this holiday. Quinn jumped up to sitting behind me, his Southern twang just barely intelligible as he was still waking up. "What in the Jesus is that shit?"

I mumbled over my shoulder. "The kids. And Christmas. When you combine the two, you get lots of yelling."

Georgia smiled at my remark and pushed a mug of hot coffee into my chest. "We better get in there before they unwrap the upholstery off the sofa."

I grabbed her by the elbow and touched my lips to her neck softly. "It is perfect, baby. You and me and the lives we created together, little monsters that they sometimes are… How could it be anything other than?"

All of her features went soft, like I'd massaged all of the tension right out of them. "Kline," she murmured, her voice mellow like her face.

"Yeah, baby?"

"Thanks for making it always hurt good."

Her words hit right me in the chest. Those were our words, ones that held a lot of memories and meaning, and all I could do was smile in response. *Ditto, baby.*

I locked my hand with hers. "I guess it's time for presents, huh?"

"You think the guys brought some of their football equipment? We might need it once the kids spot the presents under the tree…"

I laughed and let Georgia take the lead toward the impending chaos.

But before we made it to the scene of the crime—aka, the kids unwrapping presents—the doorbell rang. I thought maybe Georgie would freak out again, but she just laughed.

"I mean…who can it even be at this point?"

"My parents?" I suggested teasingly.

Her eyes narrowed dangerously, and I laughed with my hands up defensively. "Hey, you asked."

"It was a fully rhetorical question, and you fluffing know it, Kline Brooks."

"Yoo-hoo!" Dean greeted, and both of our heads turned. He was in a pose, foot turned out with one hand to his hip. After he got done posing for us, he turned to the man holding the door open for him.

Quinn had risen from his spot on the floor—though, I should have noticed the fact that I hadn't had to step over him upon exiting the kitchen—and made it to the front door before us, apparently.

"Well, hell-o." Dean looked Quinn up and down, following the lines of his sculpted body in a pair of sweat pants and a T-shirt, and then marveled over the almost perfect good-old-boy features of his face. "Sweet merciful Jesus, you're a pretty thing, aren't you?"

"Uh," Quinn mumbled and, even at the sight of an extra guest *and* all of our pets as they bounded in the door like cattle, Georgia smiled.

"Quinn, this is Dean. He works for Kline."

"For the right price, I could work for you, honey." Dean cupped his hands around his mouth and stage-whispered. "It won't cost much. Just a little slap and tickle."

Quinn's eyes widened, but it didn't last long. I expected him to turn to us for help, or even more likely, turn tail and run, but he didn't really seem all that fazed.

"Sounds like a good time, but if you want me to do any work, I cost a little more," he said in his famous Southern twang and punctuated that statement with a wink.

That wink equaled lights-out.

For real. Dean fainted.

Jesus Christ, people are dropping like flies around here...

Lucky for him, it occurred right in front of a professional quarterback with the quickest hands in the league.

Quinn looked back at us then, but we were already rushing forward.

"Come on, come on," he urged. "Help me get him to the couch."

Dean came to just as we were starting to lift, but he didn't seem shaken by his loss of consciousness in the slightest. Instead, he looked satisfied, as though he'd just lived one of his wildest Christmas fantasies to completion.

"Well, well. Merry Christmas to me, indeed."

I wasn't sure I agreed with the reasons, but the sentiment— that was worth repeating.

By the time we'd gotten Dean back to his feet and reached the tree, we found Julia and Ace jumping around the tree like banshees.

Julia twirled. "Presents! Presents! I loves everything!"

"I want to open presents!" Ace exclaimed.

"Calm down, little dude. We have to wait for everyone else to get down here," Thatch said through a yawn as he walked into the living room with Gunner on his hip. Cassie followed behind and had my daughter Evie in her arms.

"Thanks for bringing her down," Georgia said as Cassie set Evie to her feet.

Our youngest daughter didn't waste any time, running toward her sister and Ace to join in on the Christmas dance.

Wes, Winnie, and their daughter came shortly after, and the instant Julia spotted Lex, she started a whole new round of screeching and excitement.

And of course, the life of the party showed up dressed as Santa Dick with his smiling wife on his arm. "Ho! Ho! Ho! Merry Christmas, everyone! Let's see what my brother Santa Claus brought us this year!"

"Merry Christmas, Santas Dick!" Julia exclaimed. "Did you leave us some presents too?"

"Of course I did, little lady," Dick responded. "I left a few presents under the tree with your name on them."

"Yay!" Julia smiled and then looked at Savannah. "Mimi, did Santas Dick get you a present too?"

Cassie and Thatch burst into laughter, while Georgia just about choked from shock.

But Dick, well, he did exactly what you'd expect a man like Dick Cummings to do.

"Santa's dick gave Mimi lots of presents last night."

Jesus. We really need to work on the whole letter S situation.

CHAPTER 11

Let it ~~Snow~~ Go! Let it ~~Snow~~ Go! Let it ~~Snow~~ Go!

Georgia

"Good night, Julia," I whispered as I pulled the comforter over her little body and tucked her in to bed.

She yawned. And, with her eyes still closed, she offered a sleepy smile. "Love yous, Mommy. Best Christmas evers."

I kissed her forehead. "Love you too, sweetheart."

My oldest daughter was out before I walked across the room and turned out the light.

With one final glance toward Evie's crib, to find an already sleeping angel, I headed out of the girls' bedroom and shut the door.

It was official. All of the kids in the house were in bed, and thanks to Luc Marino—the chef Kline had hired to cook our meals *and* prevent me from having a nervous break down—and the five staff members who'd come along with him, the kitchen was clean and the fridge was packed full of leftovers and desserts. I smiled to myself at the idea of relaxing by the fire and headed downstairs to spend the remainder of Christmas night with the adults.

Once I reached the bottom of the staircase and walked into the living room, I found the fire aglow, the lights on the tree still glimmering, and the room filled with laughter, smiles, and that intangible feeling you can only get from the spirit of Christmas.

My parents sat together on the leather sectional, holding hands and sipping on my mother's famous boozy nog, while Cassie and Thatcher chatted about football with Cass's brother, Sean—who was currently serving as a napping spot for their pet pig, Philmore.

Winnie teased Wes about his social media skills, while Quinn Bailey and Cam Mitchell joined in on the ribbing. Stan and Walter appeared content, snuggled up together in front of the fire. And Dean was busy telling Kline about Leslie's latest ridiculous office behavior.

Everyone was here. Happy. Together.

I'd wanted this Christmas to be perfect, devoid of my crazy family's antics and set with a perfectly plotted-out itinerary jam-packed with every possible food, event, and music that signified the holiday. But as I looked around the living room filled with some of the most important people in my life, I realized that even though this Christmas wasn't perfect, *this*—spending time with the ones you loved—was what the holiday was all about.

"Georgia." Kline's voice caught my attention. "Come over here and tell Dean that Leslie isn't *that* bad."

I laughed outright as I walked over toward my husband and sat in his lap.

"Baby, I love that you try to see the best in people, but Leslie is pretty much the worst."

"Ha!" Dean smiled like the Cheshire cat. "My point exactly."

"Thanks for the help, baby." Kline just shook his head on a laugh, and I shrugged.

"That woman used to steal my lunch out of the break room. And one time, it was *cheesecake*. Believe me, after that, I will never be her number one fan."

Never steal a woman's cheesecake. If that wasn't a valuable life lesson right there, I didn't know what was.

"The girls asleep, Georgie?" my dad asked, and I realized that for the first time in the past thirty-six hours, he wasn't dressed as the infamous Santa Dick.

It was a much-needed change of scenery. Plus, I was tired of hearing Julia call him Santas Dick.

"Yep," I responded with a nod. "They were asleep before I even turned the lights out."

"Ace and Gunner were the same exact way," Cassie said and snuggled in closer to Thatch. "Christmas wore them the fluff out."

I looked across the room to my mother.

"See, Mom? It *is* possible for kids to calm down on Christmas without the need for booze," I teased, and she grinned. "Speaking of which," I added and pulled my cell phone out of my pocket. "I forgot to tell my brother Merry Christmas and that our childhood was a sham."

"A sham?" my mother snorted. "The only sham in your childhood revolved directly around that pillow you loved so much."

"Oh yeah!" my dad agreed on a chuckle. "Georgie loved that pillow. Hell, she—"

I cut him off before he got started. "Enough about the pillow, Dad!"

"Are they talking about your dirty little secret, otherwise known as your hump pillow, Wheorgie?" Cassie chimed in, and I groaned.

"I'm ignoring everyone right now."

Okay, yeah, it was true that I did, in fact, have a "hump" pillow when I was in the early years of…*discovering* myself, but that didn't mean everyone in my life needed to know about it.

But, apparently, my family and friends thought otherwise.

Those bastards were incapable of understanding personal boundaries.

Kline squeezed my shoulder, and I could feel his warm chuckles against my neck.

"It's not funny," I muttered, and he wrapped his arms around my shoulders, squeezing me tighter to his chest.

"I'm a fan of the pillow," he whispered, and I snorted.

"Yeah, and you're also a total weirdo who managed to commandeer that pillow from my parents' attic."

He just grinned, and I shook my head in amusement.

"I'm still ignoring everyone right now and texting my brother!" I announced before anyone else decided to air out my teenage dirty laundry.

"Tell Willy we said hello and Merry Christmas!" my dad exclaimed.

Me: Merry Christmas, William! Give Melody and my niece a kiss from me!

My phone buzzed with his response a moment later.

Will: Merry Christmas, Gigi. Give Kline, the girls, and our parents my love. Hope you guys are having fun at the cabin.

How did he know our parents were here? Hell, how did he even know we were at the cabin? I sure as fuck hadn't told him.

Me: Wait...what? How did you know that we were at the cabin?

Will: Because I was at Mom and Dad's the day Julia FaceTimed them from her iPad and invited them.

Oh. My. God.

My daughter. My sweet baby angel.

She was the culprit.

It was always the people you least expected, wasn't it?

Me: And you didn't think to tell me?!?

Will: I guess it slipped my mind.

Me: Uh-huh. Sure. You were probably just thankful they wouldn't be stopping by your house unannounced.

Will: Exactly.

Me: You're such a jerk.

Will: I love you too, Gigi.

Me: Pffft. Whatever. Btw Mom's eggnog is chock-full of sugar and booze. And that's not a new recipe. It's the one she has been using since we were kids.

Will: I'm well aware that Mom's eggnog has liquor in it.

What? He knew? While everyone continued to chat and laugh around me, I angrily typed out another response.

Me: Even when we were kids???

Will: Of course. Why do you think I'd beg them for more every year?

That bastard.

Me: Seriously, William? And you didn't think to tell me that either?

Will: You've always been a bit neurotic around Christmas. The spiked alcohol was much-needed to chill you the fuck out.

Me: You're the worst brother ever.

Will: I love you, Gigi.

I almost sent him a middle finger emoji, but I remembered it was Christmas. Now wasn't the time for rage.

Me: Love you too. But don't think I'll forget this conversation. And payback is the baddest chick I know...

The rage would come later.
I'd start plotting tomorrow.

Will: ☺ Merry Christmas, sis.

"Will and Mel doing good?" Kline asked as I set my phone on the coffee table.

"Uh-huh," I answered and met his deliciously blue eyes. "You know what I just found out?"

He quirked a brow. "What?"

"Guess who was the one to invite my parents to the cabin."

"Who?"

"Julia."

Kline's jaw dropped. "No shit?"

"No shit," I answered. "Apparently, she FaceTimed them from her iPad. Will just so happened to be there to hear the call."

He chuckled softly in disbelief. "Good Lord, I didn't expect that one."

"Yeah. Me either."

I guess that leaves one question unanswered...

I took a quick glance around the room and decided Quinn Bailey was my best bet on figuring out the other part of the sabotage puzzle. That insanely handsome, blue-eyed, Southern gentleman wouldn't lie.

"Hey, Quinn," I called for his attention.

"Yeah, darling?"

"Who invited you guys to the cabin?"

"Wes," he said while nodding toward the turncoat himself.

"Shit," Wes muttered and held up both hands. "I swear to God it was an accident, Georgia. I was all pumped about the win, and that ESPN interviewer asked me about my holiday plans, and it just kind of slipped. And then," he continued and pointed toward each and every one of the guys on the team, "these guys just kind of invited themselves."

"Dude," Sean chimed in, "*you* invited us."

"Yeah," Cam agreed. "You're the one who told us we could come to the cabin."

My glare returned to Wes, and he cringed.

"I'm so sorry, Georgia."

I tried to stay strong, but I could only hold that fake glare for a good thirty seconds until my face started to crack like an eggshell, and I burst into giggles.

"You're the world's worst liar, Wheorgie," Cassie announced, and I flipped her the bird.

"Hey," I started once I got my laughter under control, "I had Wes going for a little bit there. That has to at least count for something."

"You're really not pissed?" he asked, and I shook my head.

"I might've been when an extra ten mouths to feed showed up at the cabin yesterday, but no, I'm not mad now," I answered honestly. Because I wasn't mad. I was just thankful.

And blessed. So, so blessed.

"I just want you all to know one very important thing," I said and looked at each and every face in the room. "Thank you for spending Christmas with us this year. I love you guys."

Kline gave me a tight hug and kissed my forehead while everyone in the room returned their own sweet sentiments of thank yous and I love yous and Merry Christmases.

"I'd like to add something to that," Quinn announced and stood to his feet. "Thanks to Georgia and Kline's generous hospitality, this has been a fantastic Christmas. And," he added with a giant smile on his face, "it's about to be the best season for the Mavericks because we're going all the way, baby!"

"Hell yeah, boy!" Cam exclaimed, and every single Maverick in our living room hopped out of their seat and started high-fiving and cheering one another.

And I didn't care about the noise or the possibility the guys might wake the kids up.

Instead, I just savored the moment.

Life was good.

I mean, it isn't every day that a bunch of hunky, professional football players are dancing around in your living room, right?
Not to mention these guys are the soon-to-be champions...
Yeah, life is good.
Merry Christmas, everyone!

CHAPTER 12

Sleigh Ride Sleighed It

Kline

Flicking and fluttering, the flames of the fireplace in our bedroom cast a glow on the wall and wafted their heat toward us as we snuggled in bed.

Georgia sighed, and I cuddled closer, pulling her body into mine and touching our foreheads together. It'd been a long day of presents, Christmas wishes, and mayhem, and I couldn't imagine anything better than relaxing with the love of my life while the sounds of the house filtered in around us.

The kids had been in bed for a long while, but I could still hear a few chuckles drifting up from the players downstairs as they played their fifth game of poker and fell a little deeper into a bottle of scotch. Cassie and Thatch were loud enough to hear even with a room on the other end of the hallway, and the bedroom closest had Winnie and Wes, the safest choice of all the options, but that didn't mean we couldn't hear an occasional giggle.

I moved just enough to put my lips to Georgia's forehead, and she did a combination of a contented sigh and a groan.

"Something on your mind?" I asked freely, knowing Georgia liked to talk things out. I wanted her to settle. Into the bed, into happiness, and definitely into me. We had lovemaking to get to.

"Nothing really except that I guess I'll just have to try for the best Christmas ever for you and the girls again another year."

"Really?" I asked and pulled her away just enough to look her in the eye, mystified that she still didn't see it.

"Really, what?" Her thumb stroked the skin of my own, and I focused myself on relishing every stroke as I set out on my journey to explain it to her.

"How can you still not know that this year was perfect?"

She scoffed, and the covers jerked as she kicked out a leg. Obviously, our discussion was making her hot.

"Kline, come on. I had a whole plan. Traditions and memories to make. None of it happened according to plan. We didn't ice-skate or drink hot chocolate by the fire, we didn't get to go for a Christmas hike after opening presents, and I didn't get to serve you guys the roasted pork tenderloin I've been reading up on for months."

"We can skate and have hot chocolate tomorrow, and I can't wait to have the pork tenderloin one night at home. We're not hiking people, let's be real, but if your heart's really set on it, I'll make it happen. But, baby, if memories were what you were after, you got them."

"Kline—"

"No, Benny. Hear me out." I put my hands to her jaw and made her focus on me completely. "We were together, our girls were happy, and we got a whole lot of laughs out of the crazy people around us this year. To me, I'll never forget any of it. Georgie, Christmas this year? You slayed it."

"Kline—" she started, jerking her head in my hands enough

that I had to gently pull her focus back.

"Scratch that. You *sleighed* it." Her face contorted, not really with confusion, but I still felt the need to clarify. "You know, because of Santas Dick and his reindeer and shit?"

She laughed, a little crease forming between her eyebrows. "Oh yeah, I'll have memories of Santa's dick for years to come."

"All right," I groaned dramatically. "I guess, if you really need him to, Big-dick Brooks will accept the job of writing over that particular DVD."

She giggled as I rolled into her and nuzzled her neck. "Kline!"

"Wow, not even inside you and you're already yelling my name." I looked down at my cock, hanging out innocently between our bodies and already getting hard at the thought of being inside my woman, and spoke to him as though he were human. "Good job, man. You're officially in the running for a commendation."

"You're ridiculous."

I rubbed my nose against hers and hummed. "No, baby. I'm happy. Today, for Christmas, and every other day. You make me that way. You want perfect? You're it."

Her eyes grew moist as I pulled my head away from her neck and searched them.

"Kline?" she called softly. I smiled.

"Yeah, baby?"

"I guess I'm pretty awesome, huh?"

I barked a startled laugh, and she smiled, cupping my cheek with her hand.

Her voice was soft and serious as she remarked, "To land you, I'd have to be."

Is it obvious I'm the luckiest man in the world?
Because I am.
Merry Christmas, everyone!

The End ☺

Love Kline, Georgia, Thatch, Cassie, Wes, Winnie, and the
million other characters you've read about in here?
If you haven't read Thatch's bonus novella, *Mother Fluffer*, what
are you waiting for? He's just one click away!

If you're ready to dive into a whole new series of hot, sexy,
swoony male perfection, feast your reading eyes on the hottest
doctors in New York City.
The St. Luke's Docuseries will satisfy all of your romance cravings!
Start Book One—Dr. OB*scene*—today!

Plus!
Stay up to date with them and us (be the first to know about our
next upcoming release!) by signing up for our newsletter:
www.authormaxmonroe.com/#!contact/c1kcz
We've been known to get a little frisky in there, and starting
in 2018, it's GETTING EVEN BETTER—trust us, you don't
want to miss it!
Seriously, we've got BIG things coming for 2018.
You want a *tiny* hint about one *tiny* thing?
Fine. Just one thing.
Our favorite sexy football players are about to tackle love.
Trust us, there's *nothing* tiny about these guys.
Mavericks Tackle Love: Coming Early 2018.

Follow us online:

Website: www.authormaxmonroe.com

Facebook: www.facebook.com/authormaxmonroe

Reader Group:www.facebook.com/groups/1561640154166388

Twitter: www.twitter.com/authormaxmonroe

Instagram: www.instagram.com/authormaxmonroe

Goodreads: https://goo.gl/8VUIz2

ACKNOWLEDGMENTS

THANK YOU for reading. This series, these characters, have changed our lives; we hope *Sleighed It* made your holiday brighter, funnier, and gave you all the Christmas feels.

THANK YOU to our readers. We will be forever grateful for you.

THANK YOU to our tribe. The amazing people that help us, guide us, and keep our asses in line. You know who you are. We love you, adore you, and we're never letting you go—not without a restraining order anyway.

THANK YOU to our families. Thank you for understanding that when we say, "I'm almost done. Just a little more until I finish this chapter." generally means it'll be another four hours before we exit the writing cave, and we'll probably smell like BO and Cheetos dust when we do. If it wasn't for you guys, we couldn't do what we do. And then there'd be riots, obviously. So, really, you're saving mankind.

As always, all our love.
XOXO,
Max Monroe

Made in the USA
Coppell, TX
26 July 2020